The boat lurched an... powering them away from the men firing at them.

Her heart was racing, her hair was whipping around her head and she just kept them heading north from Key Largo. She knew there were some small uninhabited keys but didn't think they were large enough to provide any kind of cover.

But if she got them to Madeira Bay, Obie knew she could lose the men in the mangroves that bordered it. She might have become a city girl over the last ten years of her life, but at heart it was the swamps of Florida that she knew best.

"Keep away from other craft and the islands if you can. They had a sniper out here somewhere," Xander said.

He kept scanning the horizon, so she knew he was alert.

"I'm going to head toward the mangroves. We can ditch the boat and lose them in there."

"I'm not familiar with the terrain," he said.

"I am," she said.

Dear Reader,

I'm so excited to bring you the second book in my Price Security series. This book features Xander Quentin, who isn't exactly thrilled when his estranged brother asks for a favor. When Xander arrives in Florida, he encounters Obie Keller, whom Xander's brother also asked for help, and they are driven into the swamp and marshes near the Everglades to escape the criminal gang that's at the heart of his brother's problems.

I'm a Florida girl, born in South Florida and raised in Central Florida. I grew up on the Green Swamp, which is something I had a chance to revisit with my heroine Obie. She too grew up in the swamp and like me she got out, but there is a part of her that misses the savage beauty of it. Obie likes the woman she is now, but that swamp girl is still inside her. When she and Xander are forced deeper into the swamp, it's her knowledge of it that helps save them from nature while Xander battles the men searching for them.

I hope you enjoy this book and getting to see the Price Security team again.

Happy reading,

Katherine

SAFE IN HER BODYGUARD'S ARMS

KATHERINE GARBERA

HARLEQUIN®

ROMANTIC SUSPENSE™

Recycling programs
for this product may
not exist in your area.

ISBN-13: 978-1-335-59408-2

Safe in Her Bodyguard's Arms

Copyright © 2024 by Katherine Garbera

For questions and comments about the quality of this book, please contact us at CustomerService@Harlequin.com.

TM and ® are trademarks of Harlequin Enterprises ULC.

Harlequin Enterprises ULC
22 Adelaide St. West, 41st Floor
Toronto, Ontario M5H 4E3, Canada
www.Harlequin.com

Printed in Lithuania

MIX
Paper | Supporting
responsible forestry
FSC® C021394

Katherine Garbera is the *USA TODAY* bestselling author of more than one hundred and twenty-five novels. She's a small-town Florida girl whose imagination was fired up by long hours spent outside sitting underneath orange trees. She grew up to travel the world and makes her home in the UK with her husband. Her books have garnered numerous awards and are sold around the world. Connect with her at katherinegarbera.com and on Facebook, Instagram and Twitter.

Books by Katherine Garbera

Harlequin Romantic Suspense

Price Security

Bodyguard Most Wanted
Safe in Her Bodyguard's Arms

Afterglow Books by Harlequin

The Bookbinder's Guide to Love

Harlequin Desire

The Gilbert Curse

One Night Wager
It's Only Fake 'Til Midnight
Falling for the Enemy

Visit the Author Profile page
at Harlequin.com for more titles.

For Rob. So glad to be sharing this journey through life with you, falling deeper in love every day and finding the joy in the moment.

Acknowledgments

Growing up in the swamp and in Florida gave me such a rich setting to draw from, but my memories were that of a child/young adult. I want to thank the men in my family who helped me out with research on Key Largo and the bays that surround it.

The conversations we had in Mississippi about the unique tropical wetlands that make up the area around the Everglades were very helpful in pointing me in the right direction for research. Any mistakes are my own, of course, but thank you to Rob, Dad, Uncle Pat and Scott.

Chapter 1

Obie Keller had a soft spot for lovable losers. She didn't need to go to a therapist to know it was partially because she was still trying to save her brother, Gator, who'd run away when he was seventeen and she was sixteen. Aaron Quentin, the long-haired, tattooed dishwasher with the crisp British accent she'd hired, fit the bill of sad-luck cases. He hadn't worked for her long at the coffee shop she managed in Miami, but she liked him.

The coffee shop was owned by a Cuban American couple and was a small place in a strip mall close to Obie's house. She drove to work but could have walked if it wasn't so hot in Florida.

When Aaron had first called her from jail and asked her to get in touch with his brother and tell him Aaron needed to call in a favor, she'd agreed. But the number he'd given her was an undisclosed service that had simply allowed her to leave a message with her return number. That had been three days ago.

She hadn't heard back, and she was very afraid that Aaron was on his own. Which wasn't supposed to be her problem. He was her dishwasher, she re-drop the drug cartel speculation and concentrate on moving on so they didn't end up dead like their parents. Obie stopped trying to convince their aunt and transformed—straightened her long, curly hair and became a clone of her cousins, who were popular at the school they attended.

But Gator couldn't. He'd become more rebellious, and when he'd turned seventeen he'd disappeared. Obie had been alone since that day. Survival must have been bred into her because it was what she'd done in response. She'd graduated high school and then gone to college using the Pell Grant, receiving a degree in hospitality management. What else was she going to do living in Florida?

Outwardly, she might have looked like her aunt and cousins, but inside she was still that wild swamp girl who missed her parents.

Her aunt had since tried fixing her up with several men with good jobs. But Obie wasn't ready for marriage. She still hadn't figured herself out and didn't want to bring someone else into her bland, haunted life until she did.

She knew that the swamp girl inside couldn't survive in the real world and had resigned to leave that part of herself behind. Until Aaron Quentin showed up, reminding her so keenly of her brother that she'd wasted a few nights on internet searches trying to find him again. But there was no record of her brother.

Aunt Karen believed he must be deceased, but Obie had never allowed herself to think that. Instead, she'd always imagined he had found a better life out of Florida. She hoped he had.

For herself, she was content running the coffee shop and living in her condo a few blocks from the beach. Normally she rode her bike to work in her A-line skirt and tank top because the heat in Florida was unrelentless. But because of Aaron she was dressed up today. She drove to the jail and waited to see him.

There was something about being around police officers that always stirred memories of her dad.

She pushed them aside as she waited on one side of a glass window for Aaron to be brought in.

It was odd, but Aaron didn't seem quiet or bowed by being held. His eyes were direct when they met hers, and he seemed for a moment as if he was surprised to see her. He must have been expecting his brother.

Aaron sat down across the table from her. He was in the same clothes he'd been wearing when he'd been arrested. He had been held in the jailhouse while waiting for his bail hearing.

"Wasn't expecting to see you."

She smiled over at him. In his voice and on his face was that disappointment that she'd seen on so many faces before. Gator when he'd asked her to leave. Her aunt when she'd tried and failed to set Obie up with another guy. And now her dishwasher.

Sometimes it felt like she wasn't enough for anyone. That she always let the people around her down.

"Sorry. I haven't heard back from your brother and I think you're meant to have bail set today." Which was why she was here. She wasn't sure if she could make whatever bail that was posted for Aaron, but if she could, she'd do it immediately.

"I am," he said. "Thanks for trying."

"Oh, also I have the name of a really good pro bono lawyer. We went to school together. I wrote his name and number down for you. Maybe he can help at your bail hearing."

She pushed the paper toward him and he looked down at it, tapping it with his finger. His pinkie ring with the signet flashed before he balled his hand into a fist. "I'm good with the lawyer."

"Are you sure? You don't have to take the one they give you," she said. She had no real idea how familiar he was the criminal justice system, but she had some knowledge from her father's work.

"Yeah, Obie. Don't sweat it. I have a good attorney," he said.

"I'm glad. If you need anything at all, let me know," she said sincerely.

"Actually…" he said, pausing for a moment. "I have some information that would exonerate me, and the district attorney's office is willing to take a look at it. But I obviously can't go get it."

She wanted to believe him but didn't. He'd been arrested on drug-dealing charges, and while she'd never seen any sign of him using or selling while he'd been working for her…it was for an entire two weeks. She knew nothing about him.

That last part sounded like Aunt Karen in her mind.

"Yeah, like what evidence?" she asked. "You probably won't have to serve that much time for dealing."

"I wasn't dealing, Obie. I was gathering information on La Familia Sanchez cartel. That's the evidence I have. It's on a SD card at my place in Key Largo. If you get it for me we can show it to the district attorney."

"I'd have to talk to the district attorney's office first," she said, not sure she wanted to go out to Key Largo anytime, but certainly not in the hot summer months and not on a wild-goose chase.

"I'm meeting with them later today," he said. "Call the office and ask for Crispin Tallman."

There was an edge to Aaron's voice. But he also had a surprisingly sincere look, and she found herself nodding and agreeing to call the DA's office.

"You got a message from the service," Giovanni "Van" Price said as Xander Quentin entered the briefing room at Price Security.

Xander had been having a pretty good day. He beat Kenji in Halo, his latest client sent him a thank-you basket with his favorite protein bars and after three days off he was ready to get his next assignment and get back to work. He arrived for their daily briefing and the rest of the team was already assembled.

Price Security were an elite team of bodyguards who provided services to A-listers, diplomats and celebrities. The team was comprised of members from diverse backgrounds. Xander was the only Brit on the team and former SAS. Kenji Wada was former CIA and scary and lethal with any weapon. Rick Stone, ex-DEA agent, always looked like he needed a cigarette and was stoned or hungover, but once he was on a case, he was alert and one of the best in the business.

Lee Oscar was a seasoned intel operative for a secret organization in her past. She was cagey about admitting who it was. She was a youngish-looking forty-year-old who was their eye-in-the-sky when they were on assignment, tracking all members of Price Security and keeping them all connected when they were out. Luna Urban—currently engaged to hotshot billionaire Nicholas DeVere—was a top-notch bodyguard who'd been a MMA and street fighter before she'd joined them.

Giovanni Price was the boss of the organization and handed out the team assignments. He was short—but then everyone was compared to Xander—bald and had tattooed angel wings on the back of his neck. He went by Van and considered them all family, taking on a fatherly role, though Xander assumed Van wasn't much older than his own thirty-five years.

"I did?" Xander asked. He never got any calls. His parents sent him a card on his birthday and on Christmas and his brothers never contacted him.

They all had been changed by the accident that had paralyzed one of his older brothers, Tony, when they were young. Each remaining person in the family had taken on the blame for themselves. Xander still wasn't sure who was actually to blame. If it was him alone or all of them. Or the environment that had pitted them against each other and left them feeling like only the strongest would survive.

"Yeah. A woman named Obie Keller was calling to ask for a favor for your brother Aaron."

Hell.

Aaron was the last brother he expected to hear from. Not that he heard from any of his brothers in the last decade or so. It was just Aaron and he had the most beef with each other. The two of them had been in the SAS together, and after a particularly brutal mission they'd had a fight that had resulted in them both being discharged. But fighting was what the Quentin brothers did. They fought with each other, the world and anyone unlucky enough to cross their paths.

Aaron was eighteen months older than Xander. They had grown up rough and wild. Running all over the council estate where their family had lived. Their father was a taxi driver and amateur boxer and their mother did her best to keep them in line, changing the wallpaper and the carpet every time they were too stained with blood from the fights between him and his brothers, to be cleaned again.

Since joining Price Security, Xander had dialed that rage back by protecting those around him. He'd found his center by working closely with the other members of the team. He'd channeled some of Rick's chill, Kenji's calm and Luna's observation. They all had taught him to look outside of himself instead of dwelling on the beast inside. When he had a focus, the violence that had ruled him in the past took a back seat. "Thanks, boss."

"No problem. You're on paid leave for the next two

weeks. Think that will be long enough to take care of the favor?"

Paid leave. He really didn't want to go and see Aaron. He was still mad at his brother, and even just thinking of seeing the other man made Xander's fist ball up in his lap.

"Xander?"

"Sorry, boss. I have no idea. We're not close so… Let me check this out before you put me on paid leave."

"We'll discuss it at the end of the meeting," Van said.

Van handed out assignments to everyone but him. So he wasn't getting a job until he found out what his brother wanted. He waited until the conference room was empty of just him and his boss.

Just get up and walk out. But he couldn't. He needed an assignment. He needed something more than this shove from the universe forcing him to face his family and his past. He needed to stay busy.

Already he felt the beast inside of him stirring. Just hearing Aaron's name did that to him. Brought back the old rage and need to prove he wasn't weak.

"I'm sure the favor won't take two weeks," Xander said. "You got a job for me in Miami?"

"No."

"Why?" It wasn't like his boss to be this hard-nosed about time off. Van knew better than any of them that sometimes work was the only thing that kept them sane.

"Why what?"

"You know my history with Aaron."

"I do. I also know that you both have had time to

been told that if she was willing to wait, there might be a paralegal who could speak to her sometime that afternoon. Having already called in her assistant to cover her shift, Obie had the afternoon off.

She could have gone home and spent some quality time playing Dreamlight Valley on her Switch, pretending this never happened, but that would be selfish, and if there was the slightest chance she could help Aaron...well, she had to try.

Lost causes and all that.

Truth was, she liked trying. She just wished that one time her efforts would be rewarded. Though to be fair she had saved herself by adapting and leaving the swamp girl she'd been when her parents had died behind. Most days she didn't even remember that her hair had a tendency to curl. She used a lot of product in it and had even splurged on that Dyson hair dryer that worked miracles.

So yeah, she was the heroine of her own story...*ha*. If changing everything about herself and making herself into a bland copy of everyone else was winning, then she was definitely a champion. Maybe that was why she was trying so hard with Aaron. Gator had asked her to come with him. To take a chance on the two of them making it. And she'd been too scared to leave.

Too scared to trust him, or herself, on their own.

Even though secretly she hated everything about her new life back then, it had still been secure. She'd needed that more than she would have ever admitted to Gator. He'd gotten pissed and said a lot of mean things, called her a coward and left.

minded herself as she put on her good skirt and blazer so she'd look more professional. Obie was preparing to go down to visit Aaron and offer him the services of Adam Montel, a pro bono lawyer who she'd gone to school with.

After that, he'd be on his own.

Which of course she hated.

Aaron, with his bright blue eyes and British accent, couldn't have been further from her own brother, Gator, who'd had average brown hair and brown eyes like herself and spoke with that slow Southern accent they'd inherited from their Georgia-born mother.

Their pa had died when she'd been fourteen and Gator had been fifteen along with Mama in an airboat incident that had been ruled an accident. Something that had never felt right to Obie or her brother. Their parents had been adept at piloting airboats and at staying alive in the swamp. But the investigators said it had been due to operator error, that their parents had crashed and the airboat caught on fire, leaving them both dead.

Neither Obie nor Gator believed that. Their father had been the sheriff of their rural community near the Green Swamp in central Florida. He had been cracking down on drug traffickers using the swamp to move their product right before his death. Gator had done research once they'd been sent to live with their aunt Karen in Miami, and he was sure that La Familia Sanchez cartel had been behind their parents' deaths.

Aunt Karen hadn't been too happy to have been saddled with Obie and her brother. She'd told them to

She pulled her car into the parking lot of the building where the district attorney offices were. The address that Aaron had given her was on Key Largo as he said, but on the southern part of the long narrow Key. All the houses on Key Largo were pricey, not something that he could afford on the salary she paid him as a dishwasher.

Maybe the looming sense that Aaron had been keeping something from her was why she was reluctant to help.

But the moment the words *La Familia Sanchez cartel* had left his mouth, she was in. She didn't have to be Junie B. Jones girl detective to see that something wasn't right here.

It was scorching when she opened her door and the heat seemed to wrap around her. For a moment she was pulled back into the past and those hot, muggy summer days when she and Gator would run barefoot through the citrus grove that used to dot the landscape in central Florida. Fighting to find shade before darting into the Green Swamp and the playhouse their father had built for them up in a live oak tree.

She closed her eyes, and the longing and pain in her heart told her that unless the DA confirmed that Aaron hadn't spoken to him, Obie was going to retrieve his evidence. It might not be worth anything and might not set him free, but she would bring it to him all the same.

She pulled the strap of her large purse up on her shoulder as she headed inside. The air-conditioning brought goose bumps up her arms and legs and she almost shivered at the coolness of it as she pushed her sunglasses up onto the top of her head.

The receptionist looked up when she came in and signaled her to wait. Obie realized the woman was on the phone. When she hung up, the woman asked who she was there to see.

"I spoke to Crispin Tallman's office. They told me a paralegal might be free to speak to me this afternoon."

"Okay, what's your name?" the woman asked.

"Obie Keller."

"Okay, Ms. Keller, have a seat and I'll let them know you are here."

The office was like many of the buildings in this area, kind of comfortable but worn down from years of use. It was clear any money in the budget for updating the interior design was being spent on prosecuting cases.

Obie sat down, holding her bag on her lap because the floor looked dirty. She took out her phone but she didn't have any messages, and her socials were silent, just her looking at other people. So she put it back in her bag, noticing that the nail polish was chipped on her forefinger.

Ugh. Not going to make a very good impression with that.

But she didn't need to make a good impression, she reminded herself, though Aunt Karen said a lady always needed to.

"Ms. Keller? I'm Crispin Tallman. I was free and had some time if you'll follow me," he said.

Crispin held himself tall and with confidence. She

Crispin shrugged. "In my experience most people will say anything to get out of going to trial."

"Okay. Thanks. I'll be in touch if I find anything."

Obie left Crispin's office not confident that Aaron was going to get out of a trial...or jail time.

Chapter 2

Obie double-checked the address several times but this seemed to match the one that Aaron had given her. The houses in this neighborhood were spendy like she'd expected. But this one looked somewhat homey. Not at all what she expected someone who worked for a drug cartel to live in. In her head they were all living in a lux mansion like on the TV show *Bloodline*.

She parked her car under the car park. It was early in the afternoon and quiet. She had gone home and changed into a pair of shorts and tank top since the summer Florida heat was rising. Plus there was no one to impress on this errand she'd given herself.

What did she think she was going to find in Aaron's files? Someone who could potentially confess to having her father and mother killed, or at least being involved at the time? She knew that was unrealistic but had spent the drive down rehearsing what she'd ask Aaron if this worked out. Surely he'd have the connections to find out if the cartel had been involved in her parents' deaths.

Each of the properties was waterfront and all of them had docks behind the houses with boats in the back, including Aaron's. Having grown up in the swamp, Obie was at home on water and a part of her envied Aaron that he had this place. How *could* her dishwasher afford this place?

Crispin had said that Aaron was a drug dealer and pretty high up in the organization. She was still dealing with that reality. Her gut had been so wrong about Aaron. He wasn't a lost soul. Not at all. In fact he might be the one tempting people to leave behind their lives.

And he worked for La Familia Sanchez cartel. That was the only way he'd have evidence to get an indictment against the crime family that been notoriously hard to make convictions stick. Maybe she would get some answers about the cartel's involvement in her parents' deaths. She'd just tell Aaron that, if he wanted her to turn his evidence over, he had to tell her what he knew about her parents' deaths.

Which even in her head sounded impossible. It was a long shot, but she was definitely going to ask. She had to.

There were some lush hibiscus bushes growing on either side of the carport. The smell of the flower was so familiar. Like the heat, it wrapped around her and she was feeling nostalgic for the family she'd lost today.

This might have started out because she'd thought that Aaron reminded her of Gator, but Obie had the feeling this was more than wanting to help her brother. It felt like she was stuck in the shell of a Miami urbanite for too long—doing the right things, looking the right way but not feeling anything.

She shifted her bag from one shoulder to the other, feeling like someone was watching her. She glanced around. The road was empty.

Probably just her imagination.

She entered the house. Though Aaron had been in jail for a few days, the house was cool so he must have an automated air-conditioning system. Aaron had told her he'd hidden the files on an SD card that he'd taped under the wooden knife block in the kitchen.

She walked on the tile floors trying not to be envious and a little resentful that a drug dealer was living better than she was. Not exactly a huge surprise. But she worked hard to make ends meet and tried to bring something happy and good into people's lives…

She shook her head, trying not to get caught up in her assumptions. Aaron had made her laugh more than once. Maybe he was just as caught up in playing a role as she was.

The kitchen, like all the living spaces in this house, was on the second floor. This part of Florida was prone to flooding during hurricane season.

Aaron wasn't a bad man. Maybe he was lost, she thought, then shook her head. It would be nice to think he needed her help, that she could fix him with this one errand. But the truth was he'd probably be back to his old ways of making money. He'd probably taken the dishwasher job as a cover.

Who cared, right?

She entered the kitchen disgusted with her own conflicted feelings where he was concerned. The kitchen led directly into the open-plan living area, and there

cool down. You're not the same man who I hired nearly ten years ago."

"I don't think he's changed."

"You won't know until you go and see him. I had Lee run a search on the woman who called and your brother. He's currently in jail in Miami/Dade and she manages a coffee shop where he'd been working as a dishwasher until his arrest."

"Fu—"

"Language."

"For *fudge's* sake, seriously?"

"Yeah. Lee's sent you an information packet on the situation and all the intel we could gather. The jet is gassed and ready to go. Ping when you land and check in with Lee as you go."

"Van, this isn't a job."

"No, this is family. You know what that means," Van said as he stood and came around the table, clapping Xander's shoulder with his hand.

Van was tight-lipped about his own biological family, but Xander knew how hard the other man had worked to make all of them feel like they were one. How could he explain to Van that this found family was the only one that wanted him? That a long-ago mistake had cost him his place in the Quentin clan? And that Xander was okay with it? Because he knew that if he went back, there was a chance that he'd turn back into the rage monster he'd used to be.

Obie left the jail, driving through the midday traffic to the district attorney's office. She'd called ahead and

were floor-to-ceiling doors that overlooked the pool in the backyard and the dock with a boat on the waters of whatever bay was behind his house.

She set her bag on the counter, glancing around for the knife block but didn't see it at first. Walking around the kitchen she finally noticed a butcher block cutting board and saw the knife block next to it. Pulling it toward her, she held her breath as she took the knives out and then flipped it over.

Taped to the bottom was a small micro SD card.

That was what she'd come for. She removed it.

She heard a heavy footstep and pivoted, taking the large chef's knife in her hand as she did so. There was a huge man running toward her. She dropped the knife as she freaked out, turning to run, moving toward the door she'd come in from. She shoved the SD card into her pocket so she'd have both hands free to fight him. She didn't get very far before she was tackled to the floor.

The breath was knocked out of her by the fall, the man supporting most of his weight with his arms. He was big and hot pressing against her back. The forearm braced next to her head was thick, corded with muscles.

"Don't move if you want to live."

Her heart was racing so hard, all she could hear was the pounding of her own pulse in her ears.

"Fuck that."

She started to squirm underneath him just as a bullet hit the glass door, shattering it. The man above her wrapped his body around hers and rolled her farther from the door behind the kitchen island. He moved off of her. "Stay low."

Her hands were shaking as she watched him pull out a gun and then leaned around the island for a better position.

"Who are you?"

"Xander Quentin."

"Aaron's brother?"

"Yes. This is a fine mess. Did you get what you needed here?"

"I did," she said. "Are they shooting at me or you?"

"Well, no one saw me come in here, so I'm guessing you, Ms....?"

"Obie Keller."

"The woman who left the message for me. What kind of mess did Aaron get you into?"

Another shot was fired. He'd get to the bottom of what was going on later. First he had a job to do: protect Obie Keller and get her out of the line of fire. If he was on his own he might try to track down whoever was shooting at them. But with her at his side that wasn't an option.

He reached up to grab her bag off countertop to see if they were being watched from the back of the house. A shot hit right as he drew her bag down. She flinched.

He handed her bag to her. "Can you run in those shoes?"

She glanced down at her feet and just slipped off the flip-flops, putting them in her bag. Then she tugged the bag over her shoulder and across her body, and nodded at him.

"Which way are we going?"

"We have to get out of here—we are sitting ducks. Go to the door but keep low. I'll go first and tell you when to come. Move fast and get behind me."

She went low on her belly. For a split second the masculine part of him noted the curve of her hips and remembered how she'd felt underneath him, but he immediately shoved that aside. Now wasn't the time.

Moving cautiously, he got on his stomach, inching his way toward the door, but another shot went a little high and wide, hitting the wall next to his head, sending debris into his face and eyes. He hurried into the entryway not visible from the back of the house, rolling to pull himself out of view as more shots were fired.

He visually scanned the entire hallway. It was clear. Was there just one sniper outside? Or was he working with someone else closer to the house?

Xander estimated that the sniper to be within three thousand feet of them. And probably on a boat since all that was in the direction the shots had come from was open water, uninhabited Keys and then mangroves and the swamp. The sniper was accurate and must be well trained.

The house was quiet.

"Obie, when I tell you, run toward me," he said.

"Aren't they going to fire at me?" she asked.

"I'm going to give them a bigger target," he said dryly. He wished he had on a Kevlar vest, but hon-

could tell he commanded authority. She smiled at him. He had a pleasing face and an easy grin. His hair had been slicked back and the suit he wore was slim fitting.

"Thank you for seeing me," she said once they were in his office. They'd walked past desks with people working on files and on the computer and into an office that wasn't huge but not too small either.

"No problem. I am the assistant district attorney working the Quentin case. If he has the evidence he's hinted that he does, then I am interested in it."

"Oh, that's good. He gave me an address to go and retrieve it, but I wanted to find out what I was getting myself into."

"How well do you know him?"

"He works at a coffee shop I manage as a dishwasher," she said. "I wasn't aware about the drug dealing and I have to tell you, I never saw any of that behavior at the coffee shop."

"I'm sure you wouldn't. He's not a street dealer. Our investigation revealed he was more midlevel in the cartel. In fact, that's the only reason I'm willing to offer him a deal. If he has the information on the higher-ups, then we can talk," Crispin said.

"So what do I need to do? Get the files from his home and bring them to you?" she asked.

"Yes. The cops searched his place and didn't find anything, so I'm not entirely sure what you are going to find, but maybe you'll see something we didn't," Crispin said.

"Do you think this is a waste of time?"

estly, coming to his brother's last known address, he hadn't anticipated being shot at.

"Be careful."

"You too," he said. "Go now."

She darted out and moved quickly toward him. Her shoulder-length brown hair swinging around her face as she did so. She concentrated, her face tight with tension as she slid around him and into the hallway without a shot being fired.

"Maybe they left," she said with a hopeful note in her voice.

Doubtful. But he didn't want to scare her. He was pretty sure, given the fact that there was a trained sniper firing at them, that whoever was out there meant business.

"Or they are moving closer. Let's get out of here. I parked my rental car down the street," he said.

"My car is out front," she said, opening her big bag and digging around in it for her keys. She looked scared but game to do whatever was needed. She had on a pair of shorts that ended at the top of her thighs and a halter neck tank top that was in a bright yellow color. Not the best for blending into the environment but he'd keep her covered.

"Stay close to me. When I do this—" he held up a closed fist "—that means stop."

"Yeah, I've seen movies with that in it," she said.

"Good, then you know what to do."

He started moving down the stairs, and outside the heat wrapped around him, reminding him how much he hated it. There was a scatter of shots as two men came up the drive from the street.

Xander grabbed Obie's arm and pulled her with him as he ran around the back of the house. There was a large pool with one of those underwater pool cleaners working in it. Xander quickly ruled out making a run for another house as he heard someone approaching behind them. Xander had cased the place before he'd gone inside. He knew there was a high-powered speedboat on the dock. He had even put the key in the engine and checked that it had gas.

Xander never went into a situation without having a backup plan and it was paying off. Part of the reason why he had been reluctant to come and see Aaron was that one backup plan where his brother was concerned was never enough.

For this woman's sake, he hoped it would be today.

It was one thing for Aaron to drop him in this shit, but it was something else for him to put an innocent civilian in danger.

"We're going to take the boat and get out of here," he said. "Run toward the dock as fast as you can."

He suspected the sniper would need time to set up for another shot now that they were on ground level. The sniper was now the secondary threat, the men on foot were a more immediate danger. Everything settled around him as he focused on his mission. Protect the woman, get her to safety. That was all he would allow himself to dwell on. Later he and Aaron were going to have words.

* * *

Obie was scared out of her mind as she ran full out behind the big behemoth in front of her. Her heart was racing and she was pretty sure she was going to die. This was exactly what she deserved for stirring up the past and coming here.

The stranger might be Aaron's brother but she wasn't sure she could trust him to keep her safe. At least he was the better of the two options right now. She heard gunshots behind her and flinched as one hit the ground near her feet. She stumbled and Xander turned, scooping her up under his arm as he ran full out.

Even wearing a backpack, carrying her and returning fire didn't seem to shake him. She felt a hand on her ankle and screamed as she was jerked from Xander's arms and hit the ground hard. Her head hurt and she kicked out at the man who had her ankle.

Xander turned and dropped to one knee, firing first at the man who lunged at her, his face a mask of rage as he took aim. She heard the sound of Xander's gun and a moment later her assailant flinched and blood exploded from his chest, hitting her face and chest. Then he collapsed toward her and she pulled her leg free.

"Run to the boat—start it."

She was on the edge of panicking and completely losing it. She felt the hot tears running down her face and her hands were shaking. Xander fired another shot and then as he looked up at her, their eyes met. "I won't let them hurt you. Go now."

His words were firm and forceful. But also reassuring in a way like he'd done this before. She ran toward the boat dock. The wood was rough from exposure to the elements and she got a splinter in her heel as she ran but didn't stop.

She felt something wet on her neck and reached up to wipe it away, flinching again as she realized it was blood. For a moment the face of the man who had been attacking her flashed in her mind before she mentally shoved it away. She jumped onto the boat, which was an older-model fishing boat with a shallow bottom ideal for navigating the waters in this area. She found the key in the ignition and turned it on.

Obie pushed her hand into her pocket, double-checking she still had the SD card. Once she brushed it with her fingertips, she went and untied the mooring at the back of the boat while Xander was only a few feet away.

"Can you drive the boat?"

"Yes, just need to get that last mooring," she said, going to undo the slip knot that was used to hold it.

She hurried back to the wheel. Normally she was a slow boater observing all the no-wake zones, but with two more men running toward them and Xander providing some cover fire, she maneuvered the boat away from the dock and hit the full throttle.

The boat lurched and then got up to speed, powering them away from the men firing at them. Her heart was racing, her hair was whipping around her head and she just kept them heading north from Key Largo. She knew there were some small, uninhabited Keys but didn't think they were large enough to provide any kind of cover.

But if she got them to Madeira Bay, Obie knew she could lose the men in the mangroves that bordered it. The boat had GPS, which she looked at to make sure she was heading in the right direction. Not that she needed it in a pinch. She might have become a city girl over the last ten years of her life, but at heart it was the swamps of Florida that she knew best.

"Keep away from other craft and the islands if you can. They had a sniper out here somewhere," Xander said.

He kept scanning the horizon, so she knew he was alert.

"I'm going to head toward the mangroves. We can ditch the boat and lose them in there."

"I'm not familiar with the terrain," he said.

"I am," she said. Aunt Karen had been clear that the backwoods rural girl Obie'd been needed to disappear if she was going to make a new life for herself. But now, Obie knew that it was only the swamp girl with the skills she'd learned from both her parents that would be able to save them.

She should have known better than to get entangled in this as soon as she heard that La Familia Sanchez cartel was involved. That cartel had been responsible for driving her from her home in the swamp, and the irony wasn't lost on her that Aaron's association with them was sending her back. She'd missed her parents, her old life and had been nostalgic all day, but *this* was different. She wasn't going to just be swimming in memories but wading in the brackish water of the mangroves and swamp just like she and Gator had done has children.

"Are we being followed?" she asked.

"Probably. I don't see anyone at the moment," he said.

Time seemed to turn into this unending thing, and she had no idea if it was ten minutes or forty-five before she saw the shoreline in Madeira Bay. Xander kept watch on their back trail as she got the boat as close as she could before killing the engine.

Xander held his hand up in the stop signal he'd showed her earlier and she crouched low as he did so in case the sniper he'd mentioned was back. He took in the open water around them and then lowered his arm.

"Looks clear, but move quickly and try to present the smallest target you can," he said.

Whatever that meant. "Sure." Before she moved, she thought about the SD card in her pocket. Was it waterproof? "Uh, I have SD card with Aaron's info on it. Will it be okay if it gets wet?"

"Not sure. Watch the horizon and let me know if you see anything," he said, taking one shoulder of his backpack off and opening it. A moment later he handed her a drybag she took the SD card out of her pocket, putting it and her phone inside the drybag and then placing it in her purse.

He just watched her without saying anything. She shrugged. He said he was Aaron's brother and he had saved her, but someone was trying to kill her to get what was on that card, so she wasn't going to let it out of her sight. Her parents and even Aunt Karen hadn't raised her to blindly trust anyone.

Sure, he'd protected her from being shot, but that didn't mean she was going to simply hand over evidence that someone else was willing to murder for. She'd keep her guard up until she was safely back in her condo. Then she'd figure out what to do. If she survived that long.

She hopped over the side of the boat, feeling the warmth of the seawater on her legs up to her thighs, moving as quickly as she could until they were into the mangroves. It would be easier to swim-walk than just plain walk. She started to do some, swimming through the deeper areas, noticing that Xander did the same. She put her face in the water, exhaling, hoping it would wash away the blood and maybe when she lifted her head, she'd be at the beach in Miami and not paddling for her life near the Everglades.

Chapter 3

Once they got farther inland and out of the water, Xander looked around. The ground was sort of marshy. There was still tidal water that flowed through the roots of the mangroves. They weren't especially tall near the edge of the open water and their roots were knotted together in a kind of weave that didn't always allow for human passage between them.

Somehow Obie inherently knew which roots were pliable and moved them expertly into the mangroves, creating cover from anyone approaching from behind them. The water at his feet was getting shallower. It seemed to him that the tide was going out. He glanced up and found a spot that looked as if it might provide adequate shelter for them.

"Let's stop up ahead next to that large tree."

Obie stopped, looking over his shoulder behind him. No one was following them and they were safe for the moment.

"Should we call the police?" she asked. "I'm not even sure what to tell them. Surely the neighbors would have heard the shots by now."

"I agree. I want to check in with my boss first,"

Xander said. "We are going to need some backup if I'm going to keep you safe."

Her hands were shaking as she pushed a strand of hair behind her ear and he noticed her flinch as she looked at them. There was blood on her fingers. He could tell she was scared but she must have a core of steel. She'd done what was needed to get them away from the house and through the mangroves to relative safety. While bleeding as an innocent civilian.

Damn.

"Let's get you cleaned up," he said.

She just nodded again. Was she going into shock? He wouldn't blame her. He had some mental health training because of his line of work, but his skill set was more to defend and protect someone than to counsel them after an incident. But he had to do something. If she lost it then his swamp expert was gone, and they were both good as dead.

One of the things Van always said was *When you don't know what to do, do what you know.* She knew this area so maybe talking about it would give her something to concentrate on. "So you said you know the swamp?"

He shrugged out of his pack and pulled out some wet wipes that Lee insisted they all carry in their go bags. He stood up and held it out to her. She took it and cleaned the blood from her arms just as he noticed a cut near her temple. She must have gotten hit by some shrapnel when the sniper had nicked the counter near them.

Using an antiseptic wipe this time, he cleaned around

the wound. She tipped her head toward him as he treated her. He had some antiseptic strips that he put on the wound to close it and hopefully protect her from infection.

"The swamp?" he asked again.

She licked her lips and chewed on her bottom one for a moment. He couldn't help noticing that she had full lips and a very kissable mouth.

Not that it mattered, as he definitely wasn't going to be kissing her. She was a client now. And they were still on the run.

"Yeah, until I was fourteen, almost fifteen, I lived in the swamp with my parents," she said. "So I know how to navigate it. I mean I grew up in central Florida, and the Green Swamp has a different ecosystems than the Everglades, but hopefully I have enough knowledge to keep us safe. I've read some stuff on the Everglades after moving here."

"You're doing great," he said, putting on the bandage. She was calmer now. Talking was helping.

He was also intrigued by her story. Why had she left the swamp? What was she doing in Miami if she was from central Florida? Mostly he liked the sound of her voice and realized her talking was calming him down as well.

Of course conversation and small talk weren't his thing, and right now he was dealing with keeping his anger at his brother in check, trying to figure out the situation they were in. He took Van's advice for himself. Focus on the mission and not on his stupid AF brother. "Catch me up on everything that Aaron told you?"

"Don't you know?" she asked, flinching back away from him. "How else did you know to come to the house?"

"Your message just said he was in jail and needed a favor. I figured I should start with his place to gather intel."

She shook her head. "Can I see some ID? I mean, you saved me from being killed and you have a British accent, but I'm still not sure…"

He got it. Her questions were logical. Xander knew his brother, and the kind of trouble Aaron was in would attract many enemies and require elite training. He pulled out his wallet, handing it over to her. He had nothing to hide and honestly, seeing her still shaking and scared and looking at him with suspicion made him want to do everything he could to reassure her.

He was going to punch Aaron in the face when he saw his brother for putting a civilian in the middle of this mess.

She took his wallet and pulled out his ID and the photo he'd forgotten he'd wedged behind it. She shifted the two things in her hand and her eyes went to the picture. He turned away knowing what it would show. Himself and Aaron in the middle, Abe and Tony on either side. It was taken the day of the accident that had changed all of their lives. They were all standing tall, posturing to show which was the biggest and strongest. Turned out none of them were.

"Okay, sorry about that, you're definitely Aaron's brother." She put the ID and picture back into his wallet before handing it back to him.

"I think we should call the cops," she said again. "But you wanted to call your boss. What is it you do?"

"I work for Price Security. We're a private body-guard firm."

"That explains the gun and your skill with it," she said. "Call your boss if you want, but I'm going to try the police."

She pulled her phone out of the drybag he'd given her, scowling as she realized there wasn't a cell signal. "My phone's useless."

"Mine won't be. It's a satellite one. Let me call my boss and *then* we can call the cops," he said, admiring the face that she was take charge. He shouldn't have been surprised based on how she'd behaved since the moment they met. The cops couldn't do much to help them, but he knew that it would make her feel better to call them.

Unless they were in on it too. The cartel's influence was clearly wide, and corrupting local law enforcement was a common tactic.

He turned on his phone and put his earpiece in. He hit the Price Security button and Lee was in his ear in a moment.

"What's up? Enjoying the sun and sand?"

"Not exactly. Someone just shot up Aaron's place. I'm with Obie Keller," he said.

He heard Lee's fingers moving on her keyboard; she was already locating him and doing a search on Obie.

"Gunfire was reported in Key Largo at your brother's last known address. Police dispatched. An alert is out for a man matching your description and a woman with brown hair, slender build. They want you for questioning. An eyewitness IDed you as the shooter of the deceased," Lee said.

"Fu—"

"Language," Lee said with a smile in her voice. "But yeah. I think you should get some cover. I'll dig and find out a safe place for you two to turn yourself in for questioning."

"Obie's been speaking to someone in the district attorney's office. They would be a good contact. Aaron has information that is going to be used in a case against La Familia Sanchez cartel. That means she has a target on her back now."

"She does, and so do you. That information is good to know. What do you need from me to keep her safe?" Lee asked.

"We are going to need extraction. We had to abandon the boat and we are hiding in some mangroves," he said concisely. Getting to a safe house would be the easiest thing at this point.

"I'll start working on it," she said, and he heard her fingers moving on her keyboard. "What's the contact's name?"

"Who were you talking to at the district attorney's office?" he asked Obie.

"Crispin Tallman. He is an assistant district attorney working Aaron's case, and he's willing to cut a deal depending on the quality of the information," Obie said to him.

He nodded and relayed the information to Lee. "I'll check in with him. If you head west, northwest you should hit Cuthbert Lake. I'd stay south and go around it. Just past it is West Lake and on the far west side there is a marina. Head that way and I'll dig up info, check in when you are there."

"Will do. Bye."

"Bye, X. Stay safe."

Obie arched one eyebrow at him. "What is going on?"

He caught her up on what Lee had told him as he dug out his first aid kit. A bullet had grazed his left bicep, and now that Obie was safe, Xander was ready to clean it.

"The cops want to talk to us?"

"According to what Lee heard. You said you got an SD card and that Tallman and Aaron were the only two who knew you'd be there?"

She gave a short nod and licked her full, rosy lips. She pushed her sunglasses up to the top of her head. "Let me help you with that wound."

She bandaged him up and then turned away, going around the side of the tree. Her breath came out in a ragged sigh as she sank to the ground, pulling her knees up to her chest.

Xander stood there unsure how to help. Protecting her from an assailant with a gun or knife he could handle, but managing emotions and a creeping attraction to his charge…not so much.

Her arms wrapped around her body, Obie held herself tightly. She'd been on her own since Gator had left, but the world that he'd abandoned her in had been one that was easy to adapt to. It had been boring, but safe. It wasn't that she had wanted to be on her own, but the promise of safety…she hadn't felt safe after her parents' deaths.

This was something else.

She hadn't heard gunfire since they'd left the swamp. Hadn't been shot at ever, and she was freaking out. They couldn't go to the cops, according to the behemoth, and she was putting her faith in the brother of her jailed dishwasher. She truly had no idea who that man was. She couldn't even remember his first name, though she'd knew he'd given it to her when they'd been crouched behind the desk.

God, that felt like a lifetime ago.

"You okay?" he asked.

"Yeah." No. She wasn't ever going to be okay again. But a part of her knew that was a lie. She had felt the same when her parents had been killed and she and Gator had been sent to live with Aunt Karen. She'd adapted and she'd learned to survive. Now she was going to have to dig deep and push past emotions she'd repressed for so long, telling herself she was fine. But fine wasn't going to cut it in the swamp. She was going to have to be her true self and she wasn't sure she was ready for that.

She had this, she told herself. Except someone had freaking shot at her and she could still feel that man's hand wrapping around her ankle. Her entire body ached from hitting the ground and she felt like…well, she'd never be safe again.

Her breath started to become more rapid and she felt her heart racing. She was having a panic attack.

Damn. She hadn't had one since she'd first come to live with Aunt Karen.

"Hey, you're okay. I'm not going to let anyone or anything get to you," the behemoth said.

"Yeah."

"Why are you doing this?" he asked.

"Doing what? Also what's your name? Sorry, I've forgotten it. I mean I know I just read it on your ID and everything."

"It's okay. I'm Xander. I'm a bodyguard," he reminded her with a gentle smile.

Bodyguard. Well, that explained his muscled frame and why he had put himself between her and the men firing at them so many times. Also he had a calm surety about him that made her feel like he'd be able to handle anything that came at them. He had carried her and taken down a man attacking her at the same time, so she wasn't even exaggerating that.

"I'm not sure either of us is safe. Do you think that the men were with La Familia Sanchez?"

"Yes. I'm more concerned about how they got our descriptions to law enforcement so quickly. I think we need to try to read whatever is on the SD card you picked up. What did Aaron say the evidence was?"

"He didn't. But Crispin—that's the assistant district attorney—said something about evidence to convict people higher up in the cartel."

"That's right. Evidence that has put your life in danger. Aaron never should have sent you to collect it," Xander said.

"I think he was hoping his brother would show up and he wouldn't have to ask me," she said pointedly.

"Yeah, I'm sure he was," he said in a biting way, and then he glanced at her and something changed in him. He scrubbed his hand over his face and shook his head. "I am sorry you were caught in the middle of this."

He pulled a bottle of Gatorade from his pack and twisted off the cap, offering it to her. She took it and, even though she wasn't a fan of the beverage, took a long swallow. She didn't want to chance getting dehydrated. He took another bottle and drained it one long gulp.

She looked at him, really *looked* at him, for the first time, noticing that he was an attractive man. She had seen the photo of him with his brothers and there was a similarity between him and Aaron, but they were also very different. They both had that same thick hair that tended to curl, but where Aaron's was brown, Xander's was black. They both had blue eyes, but Aaron's always seemed to hold a hint of laughter and Xander's... well, didn't.

There was a seriousness to him and a calmness that made her feel safe. Guess that was something he'd had to cultivate as a bodyguard. As he put the empty bottle back in his pack, her eyes drifted lower, to his lips. He had a full mouth, and she couldn't help staring at it for longer than she should.

He arched one eyebrow at her and she shook her head. "Why didn't you call me back?"

Something like anger, or maybe just annoyance, seemed to pass over his face. She was pretty sure he wasn't interested in discussing this with her. But if she didn't keep talking, she was either going to throw herself at Xander and kiss that tempting mouth of his, or she was going to let go of the control she was barely holding on to and completely freak out.

"If you had, we might not be standing here in the mangroves with the cops wanting to talk to us," she pointed out.

God, she sounded like Aunt Karen. Carefully assigning blame with a side of guilt to get what she wanted. She didn't like that side of herself.

"Fair enough. Things are complicated with Aaron. We aren't close and haven't really been in touch for years," Xander said.

He turned to face the water in front of him and she confronted the cut on his face again. He seemed invincible, and she'd cleaned the bullet wound on his arm so she *knew* he wasn't, but seeing the cut on his face was another reminder. Even this larger-than-life man was human and fragile, just like her. "I'm sorry to hear that."

"Are you close to my brother?" he asked.

She felt close to most people she worked with. Probably because they all had to have each other's back during the morning and lunch rush. She had to rely on her staff to get things done and they all bonded over working hard together. It wasn't something she could explain. Aaron had made her laugh during their downtimes while he washed the dishes and they'd reset for the next rush.

She'd thought…that she knew him. Never guessed

that he was hiding anything. Which was her bad, really. She spent most of her time pretending to be someone she'd had to become, so it was silly that she wouldn't have recognized the same qualities in him. But she hadn't. Part of assimilating into a clone of her cousins and aunt was expecting that everyone was normal. In her job she took people at face value. Clearly she shouldn't have done that with Aaron. She'd let her guard down and look where it had gotten her.

"He started working for me a few weeks ago," she said at last. "So no. Not close at all."

"Yet you risked your life for him."

When he put it like that, he must suspect she had another reason for helping Aaron. She just didn't know him well enough to really understand what he was thinking and what he might believe of her. Did she want to mention her own muddy past with La Familia Sanchez cartel? No. And she didn't know Xander well enough to trust him with that. Not yet.

"I mean I thought I was picking up a file and driving it back to Miami, which isn't really risky."

Xander gave her a half smile. "Guess today wasn't what you planned."

"Nope."

"Nothing with Aaron ever is."

"Really?"

"Yeah. I mean maybe that's the way it is with all siblings. I'm not really sure. Me and my brothers have a very difficult way of dealing with each other," he said. "You have any?"

"Um, I have a brother. That relationship is complicated too," she said. "Actually, Aaron reminds me of my brother."

Something rustled in the underbrush behind them. Xander pulled her to him, maneuvering her so that her back was against the tree and his body was pressed against her front. He was so close that she felt his exhalation against her cheek. Her lips parted and her body was once again making her very aware of Xander.

She felt her lips slightly tingle. This was a bad idea. She glanced over his shoulder and saw a small opossum scurrying from one bush to another. She should definitely not be checking out Xander while they were in the swamp with the cartel after them.

But it seemed being in the heat and the isolating swamp was stirring up all of her instincts, including the feminine ones she always ignored. She wanted to shake herself. Now wasn't the time to finally be attracted to a man.

Xander noticed it too and relaxed his grip on her, stepping back and shoving his hand through his hair. She missed his touch for a moment before she mentally gave herself a smack. *Snap out of it!*

"Aaron's an idiot. He knew I'd come. He just was impatient like always. He had no business putting you in danger."

"Thanks," she said. "But I volunteered."

"You said he reminds you of your brother. How?"

"Just lost. Like he needed someone to look out for him," she said. Not really sure why she was admitting this to a stranger. But the truth was she no longer was sure of anything. Being shot at, being in a boat traveling at high speeds across the Florida Keys. It stirred that long-ago girl she'd been, the one that craved adventure. Made her question all the changes she'd made to fit into a world that had never been her own.

Plus she still wasn't sure of Xander's motivations. He hadn't responded when his brother had first reached out and now he was here. Something must have changed his mind.

"Does it help with your brother?" he asked. "Because I've taken the opposite tack with Aaron and it's not really working."

"Well, I haven't seen Gator since I was sixteen. I didn't look out for him back then."

She heard the sadness in her own voice. This afternoon had made a mess of all the control she'd normally used to get through her day.

She looked up, and her eyes met Xander's blue ones. She was tempted to tell him about her parents and the information she was hoping to get from Aaron, to see how far trust could go, but instead she just wrapped one arm around her waist. "A part of me is trying to correct the scales and bring some balance. Maybe by helping your brother I can make up for not helping mine."

He put his hand on her shoulder and squeezed. A tingle of sensual awareness went through her.

"You've made up for it," he said.

"I don't think you get to decide that," she said. "I haven't really done much."

"Except drive a long way to get some info that may keep Aaron from jail. I'm not sure what you didn't do for your own brother but I think that counts. Plus you were shot at and you got us to safety."

"You make it seem like I saved the day when we both know it was you."

He put his hand under her chin. "You did a lot more than you realize."

Their eyes met and something passed between them. That awareness that had been stirring between them earlier was back. She let her eyes drift down to his mouth and then half closed them as he brought his mouth down toward hers.

Chapter 4

Xander wanted to blame the heat, or the adrenaline, or the fact that he was in party-centric Miami for almost kissing Obie, but he knew that the cause was the woman herself.

She tempted him. There was something about her resilience and the way she'd handled herself under pressure that got to him. Being so big, everyone just let him take control, but with Obie he could tell she was used to relying on herself, keeping control. He lifted his head and saw the same confusion coursing through him on her face.

He wanted to say something, knew that he should, but he had no words. Talking about anything had never made things better for him. He screwed up when he spoke.

Instead he leaned into what he did best—protecting her. He heard the sound of a boat motor coming toward the area where they'd ditched their boat earlier.

Damn. Had someone been watching them the entire time? They weren't exactly in deep cover, but even a seasoned tracker would have had trouble spotting them in the clutter of mangrove roots.

"We need to hide," he said. He wasn't sure how many men were in the boat that was following them or even if the boat was after them.

She gave him a tight nod. "I think if we go further into the mangroves until they pass it might give us the advantage."

"You know the swamp better than me," he said.

Her hair had started to curl as they stood in the humidity of the Florida summer day.

He regretted not kissing her for two reasons: one, he could see that she'd needed some kind of human touch. After being shot at and chased he totally understood where she was coming from. Adrenaline and fear had a comedown and human contact was the easiest way to manage it.

The second was that he needed it too.

She gestured for him to follow her. Before he did, he pulled her close and gave her a rough hug. He wasn't a physical person except for sex, which to him was a physical need, not something involving emotions. So comforting her wasn't something that felt natural, and the hug probably wasn't the best. But she gave a ragged sigh and then half smiled up at him.

That smile went straight to his groin…and something deeper. But he didn't want to be reacting to her emotions while he was turned on and they were fighting for their lives. The two weren't meant to go together. At least not for him.

"We're going to get wet again," she said.

"As much as I'm sweating I won't mind it," he said dryly.

She lead them farther away from the open water and the tree they'd taken shelter behind. The ground turned marshy and then it deepened into the brackish mangroves. She led them to the relative shelter of a large mangrove and then slipped under the branches, bringing him with her.

They heard the other boat slow, riding the edge of the mangroves. From his position it was hard to make out the features of the three occupants on the boat. They had guns and were using binoculars to scan the shoreline.

"Can you hold your breath?" he asked.

"Yes."

"Big breath and then under when I tell you," he said.

Her eyes went wide and then she nodded. He waited until the boat got closer to where they were. "Now."

She took a deep breath, as did Xander, and they both ducked under the water. The SAS training he'd had was a bit like the US Navy SEAL training, so he could hold his breath for almost three minutes. But he hoped it wouldn't be that long. He couldn't expect her to do this for hours on end; she was a civilian.

Obie put her hand on his arm and he turned toward her. Due to the sunlight he had a partial view of her face. Her eyes widened and she pointed behind him. He glanced over his shoulder to see an American crocodile swimming toward them.

Of course it was.

There was something in the cold eyes of the crocodile as it moved through the water. The predator in him recognized the same in the animal.

God damn his brother straight to hell. He'd known. Known the moment that he'd heard Aaron's name that this was all going to go to shit.

Xander had never confronted a croc. His training in the mountains of Wales strangely hadn't gone into detail on crocodiles. Somehow the idea of actually facing one on a mission seemed too ridiculous to be real.

Obie just squeezed his wrist, bringing his attention back to her.

Stay still, she mouthed to him.

He gave a quick nod of his head.

He had almost forgotten about the threat from the men following them as the crocodile got closer. It crept slowly toward him, its eyes moving over them. The closer it got, Xander could clearly see the teeth. He'd read once that crocodiles submerged their prey and took them into a death roll, suffocating them. Or was that an alligator. Hell, he couldn't remember.

But the crocodile slowly swam right on past them. As soon as it departed, Obie gestured for them to surface.

Slowly, she mouthed again.

He moved as carefully as he could, keeping one eye on the retreating croc, and then as his head broke the surface, he emerged only to his nose. The sound of the boat was gone but he wasn't taking any risks.

He scanned the edge of the mangrove swamp and noticed that the craft was gone. Obie had surfaced next to him. She was watching the direction the crocodile had swum in.

"Can we move?" she asked, her voice pitched low.

Given that they were facing danger on two fronts, he knew she didn't mean for the low timbre of her voice to be sexy. But it was. It was hard not to be attracted to a woman who'd kept her cool the way that Obie had. She surprised him. Something that rarely happened.

"Yes. Slowly. Stay low," he said.

"Get back on land," she said. "Crocs are fast on land so we don't want to catch his attention."

"Got it."

He led them from the shelter of the mangrove branches back the way they came. As they got back on the marshy land, he checked his compass and went in the direction that Lee had suggested. Obie was moving quietly behind him. She touched his waist at one point and he paused, glancing over his shoulder.

"I think we're clear now. From the croc anyway."

"That's good. I think the men chasing us are gone for now too," he said.

"Yeah? That's a relief. Do you think they'll be back?" she asked.

"Probably. I mean they were gunning hard for you. And I killed one of them…so yeah, I don't think they are going to just walk away."

"I was afraid of that," she said, tucking a strand of hair that had escaped her ponytail back behind her ear. "I wonder if I should use your phone to call the district attorney. Maybe if we get the SD card to them… But how are they going to stop La Familia Cartel from coming after us? If that even was them, but given that they have eyes and ears everywhere…"

Xander couldn't help smiling at the way she listed

options and then ruled them out. Strength was something he was drawn to. Obie had been thrust into this situation and she wasn't cowering and waiting for him to take the lead. "Exactly. The company I work for has a lot of connections. I think if we go to this marina they suggested, that will give them time to get some intel and us some time to recoup from being shot at. It's not my favorite thing."

She looked back over her shoulder at him. "I'd be worried about you if it were."

He cracked a smile and shook his head. "Me too."

"Why are you and Aaron in the US instead of still in jolly old England?"

She attempted a bit of a British accent on the jolly-old-England bit but sounded more like Paul Rudd in the movie *Forgetting Sarah Marshall* than like a true Brit. "Can't speak for Aaron as I didn't realize he'd come over here. But I was recruited by Van Price to join his security team after I left the SAS."

"What's the SAS?"

"Special Air Service. Sort of like your Navy SEALs." He'd needed to find a reason, a purpose for the big muscles and the strength that had always been a part of him. A way to try to make sense of his desire for strength instead of succumbing to the insecure destructive side that had led to one of his brothers being paralyzed. Joining the SAS suited him.

"Did you have to do a bunch of extreme stuff to prove yourself before you become one?" she asked.

"Yeah, some. Aaron was actually in my class."

"Really? I wouldn't have guess that about Aaron.

He's so chill and laid-back, but then I didn't know him the way I thought I did," she said, chewing her lower lip between her teeth and taking a deep breath.

"We both changed after the SAS. We had a falling-out and he went his own way. The man you know might be the result of the last ten years." He didn't let himself dwell on the emotions he still hadn't dealt with from that last fight with Aaron. It was past time to try to make amends, but he hadn't known how.

She wrapped one arm around her waist as a tepid breeze blew around her, making her ponytail sway. "Has it been that long since you've seen him?"

"Yeah."

He wanted to reassure her that Aaron wasn't using her, but that was more down to the woman Obie was. He wanted her to keep her faith in people. From Xander's experience, he didn't think he would be able to trust his brother. Aaron had gone rogue from life. Xander had seen it firsthand.

"Is that why you hesitated to come and help him?"

He shrugged. As much as he wanted to reassure Obie, he really wasn't into disclosing any part of his past. Partially because he was now thinking of himself as her bodyguard and he didn't want to blur the lines between personal and professional. Their attraction was already threatening that carefully made boundary. "It's complicated."

"Yeah, whatever, you said, but since we have a long walk and I don't want to keep reliving the memory of that guy who grabbed me…maybe you can talk to me about something sort of normal."

She turned away from him. The sun was hot and he felt that heat all the way to his bones.

Something primitive stirred deep inside of him and he was seconds away from just letting loose, relinquishing his control. He couldn't close his eyes and meditate, not while they were walking and the cartel was on their back trail.

He looked back at her. She had said *whatever*, like she thought he was copping out of admitting the truth.

"Things between me and Aaron are complicated and neither of us has ever talked about it. I'm not sure I can put it into words. But he was once my best friend and then everything changed. I blame myself and him for what happened but we don't talk to each other."

She barely nodded. "Why not?"

"Why not what?"

"Why don't you talk?" she asked. "Not that it's my business. I shouldn't be pushing you."

"I suspect you are trying to figure out what Aaron got you into and if he's worth it."

He paused to see if he was right. He wouldn't blame her for staying focused on getting out of the swamp and not really caring too much about Aaron or himself. She chewed her lower lip again and gave a half nod.

"*I don't know* is the short answer. The brother I knew was a man of honor and had a strong moral code. But it's been ten years—that might have changed," Xander said.

"Have you changed in the last ten years?" she asked.

"I have."

"And?"

"That's why I'm not sure. Life had required sacrifices from me that shifted the man I used to be. I haven't compromised or done the easy thing to stay comfortable, but that's not my way."

She shook her head. "This isn't helping."

"I know. I'm sorry. I hate getting into my feelings."

They continued walking. This situation wasn't what he'd expected and frankly he'd been expecting it to be pretty damned complicated and difficult from the beginning. Confronting the ghosts of the past was something he'd never thought to do in this situation, at least not with a beautiful stranger while his wayward brother was in prison.

He wanted to protect Obie. Maybe if he made her his job then he could get them both through this without having to deal with too much fallout from Aaron and his involvement with La Familia Sanchez cartel.

"What's next?"

"We've got about thirty more minutes until we reach the first lake. I have a pack-raft in my bag that we can use when he get there. It self-inflates so we'll take another little break. But going across Cuthbert Lake instead of around it should save us a lot of time."

Because if he didn't think of Obie as a client, as someone he needed to protect, he was very afraid he'd open that tight control he'd always kept on himself.

The one thing he tried to never do was lie to himself.

It was her. She was making things complicated for him. Complicated in a way that he wasn't sure he could control.

* * *

Obie wasn't entirely sure why she'd almost kissed him. She could say it was from relief, and of course it *was* the first time she'd been shot at. She'd been around guns all her life—all her early life. Living in the swamp necessitated knowing how to shoot a rifle to keep snakes away from their house. But she'd never been shot at, never faced the barrel of a gun head-on… It was still freaking her out.

Being on the water had always been something that soothed her, but walking through the swamp was stirring so much anxiety. She was having a bit of a panic attack just remembering Xander running toward her, then the bullet hitting the glass in the room.

The sun continued to blaze and she thought about the croc they'd seen. She'd been anything but chill when she first noticed it, but then she heard her daddy's voice in her head telling her most swamp creatures weren't out to attack. Just sort of inhabited a live-and-let-live attitude. It had been years since she'd allowed herself to think of her parents, much less hear their voices.

But walking through the swamp was something they'd done together so many times, it was almost as if she could feel them walking beside her.

She'd shut out so much when she'd landed at Aunt Karen's and had to figure out how to survive in a world that wasn't her own. But today she realized how much she'd lost when she'd done that. This was life-and-death and she had no choice but to use her swamp skills.

The shocking thing was that she still liked it. Loved

it. And she didn't have to hide her knowledge from Xander.

"You okay?" he asked after about fifteen minutes of walking.

No.

She was pretty sure she wasn't going to be okay until she got rid of the SD Card that Aaron had sent her to retrieve. But Obie forced a smile and nodded. "Yeah. Just hot."

The man was big and built. His shoulders were large, like Captain America when he was trying to keep Bucky from taking off in the chopper in *Captain America: Civil War.* She had no business checking him out but it was hard not to notice. He was also *tall.* Much bigger than Aaron, probably by about three inches in height and maybe twenty pounds in muscle.

Xander glanced over his shoulder at her and behind her dark sunglasses she felt safe letting her gaze move over that big body of his. She felt safe with him. Having him by her side with skills that she, as a basic manager of a coffeehouse, didn't have was reassuring.

"You probably want to put on some sunscreen," she said, realizing he was starting to turn a little bit red. She dug around in her purse until she found the small container she always carried.

He arched one eyebrow at her but took the container she handed him.

"Thanks."

Smiling at him, she had a moment where she felt like she was living someone else's life. "This is just so weird."

"Yeah, it is. I don't know how my brother got mixed up with a huge drug cartel."

"It's so hard to really know someone. Even when you live with them all the time," she said. "I guess ten years would make you more like strangers."

Xander didn't say anything as he poured the sunscreen into his hand and rubbed into his arms and then his neck and face. "We were strangers long before that."

She thought about her own relationship with Gator. She knew exactly what it was like to have that distance with a sibling. The only thing she wasn't sure about with Xander and Aaron was if one of them had regretted it. The way Xander was acting, she was pretty sure there was unfinished business between them. She'd regretted the distance between herself and Gator but she had never been sure if he regretted it too.

A part of her had reignited hope for an answer since the moment she'd heard La Familia Sanchez had wanted to find answers about her parents' deaths. As if in some way that would bring Gator back into her life or fix that broken past.

Xander didn't want to talk about his estrangement with Aaron in the middle of hiding from killers in a swamp. But it wasn't only Obie making him think of his brother. He'd been inundated with memories since Van had brought his name up in the staff meeting.

Why now?

And what exactly was this mess Aaron was in? Seeing his brother as a midlevel drug dealer made no sense. The house he'd gone to wasn't something a low-level dealer or dishwasher in a coffeehouse could afford. Also given the fact that the cartel had been watching the house, he believed the information that Aaron had was very valuable.

He looked over at Obie. She'd pulled her hair back into a ponytail but a few wisps still flew around her head. He had the coordinates on the map on his satellite phone but the geography here was foreign. He was drowning in this assignment. Which wasn't even an official assignment. Lee had sent him a list of bars and clubs to check out so he could relax when he was in Miami prior to landing, thinking bailing Aaron out of jail and getting to the bottom of things would take no time at all.

Now Lee'd updated his phone with information on poisonous snakes and plants to watch for as well as the coordinates to the area she wanted him to head to.

No one had anticipated this. But Xander should have. He knew Aaron; his brother wouldn't have reached out unless he was out of options. But Xander also inherently believed his brother was still a good person. So that meant he needed to read whatever was on that SD card and get more information about what exactly his brother had been up to.

"You said Aaron hadn't been working for long..." He sort of tossed it out as a question.

"Yeah, almost three weeks," she said.

"Did you notice anything about him?" he asked.

She licked her lips. "Nothing unusual. He got to work early, was a very efficient dishwasher and liked to flirt with everyone who came into the shop. He didn't hesitate to jump in and do any task that needed doing. Honestly I thought he was a really good worker. He seemed a little too educated to just be washing dishes," she said.

"In what way?"

"Just that I could tell he'd done higher level work," she responded.

"Why did you hire him?"

She took a deep breath. "Everyone needs a second chance. He was vague about his references and what he'd been doing previously but it seemed to me that he needed work. So I took a chance. And until today I didn't have any second thoughts about him."

Sounded like the brother he'd known. All of the Quentins had been raised to work hard. Everyone pulled their own weight and there was no job that was too small for any of them. A part of Xander was glad to hear his brother still had that work ethic.

He wanted to ask her more questions but before he could, she spoke.

"You said you're a bodyguard. What's that like?" she asked.

He shrugged. "I don't know. It's a job. I get a mission brief, I protect my client for the duration of the contract and then I go back to LA until my next assignment."

She shook her head. "I have a job. What you do is something you chose. A vocation or a lifestyle or something."

"Or maybe it chose me," he said without really thinking. After his brother's accident Xander had to tame his own strength and learn to use it to keep others safe. The path stretched in front of him before he could know anything else.

"You always wanted to protect others?"

Shielding people from harm hadn't been on his mind until the accident. It was Obie who was stirring up all of his instincts in that department, and probably more than a little residual anger toward Aaron that was making him so protective of her.

The rage and the violence inside of him was once out of control. All of the Quentins were used to fighting; punching, blood and gore was a part of their everyday life. And being the best was what they'd all been striving for, until that moment when…everything had changed.

He knew that protection was a means to the only end he could live with. He had to protect because that was the way his strength could serve others and control that beast deep inside of him. He was disciplined not because he liked order but because if he wasn't then no one was safe.

"Yeah, I guess so. I mean my dad was in the military so we grew up roughhousing." Even as the practiced words came out of his mouth he regretted them. He'd heard his mom use that excuse about the violence in their home and it had become his pat answer. But the truth was they'd been allowed to run wild and no one had ever tried to stop them.

Obie was making him very aware of the man he'd been and the man he was trying to be. She'd put her life in his hands whether she knew it or not. And the fact that Aaron had put her in danger made this more personal than Obie would ever know. But he wasn't going to let anyone hurt her, not the men who were after them and not the beast inside of him.

"You look very intense," she said.

Well, hell. He didn't know any other way to be, he guessed. "Yeah that's my resting face."

"Yeah? Mine is sort of bitchy so I have to remind myself to smile all the time. You should do that too."

He looked at her, not sure but...he thought she was teasing him. No one ever did that. He always thought it was his intimidating size. Some people called him a giant or goliath and he shrugged it off. He was sort of a half giant. He gave her a fake half smile, half smirk.

God, he felt so weird and awkward. Why was he trying to smile?

A genuine grin flashed across her face and she laughed. "Ya need practice."

"Ya think?"

"I do."

He was tired of being in his head and in the past. He wanted to know more about this woman who'd taken a big risk even if that hadn't been her intent when she'd come to help out his brother. She fascinated him. Even though she really shouldn't, given they were in the swamp and bad guys were chasing them. But nothing about today was normal.

"So Obie... That's an interesting name..." He just left that statement there. Wanting to talk about her and not his brother or the mess they were in.

"It's different, isn't it? It's a nickname. My parents named me Orange Blossom but always just called me Obie."

"Ah, I'm Alexander," he said. "Not sure why." Orange Blossom. It was something he associated with Florida and actually looking at her. She was very much a Florida woman. At ease in the sun and on the water.

Her name suited it because it was distinctly unique just as she was. Reminding her that she was in danger should have been his priority, but instead he couldn't help watching her move through the swamp with a natural grace and instinct. All he could think was that he'd gotten lucky Aaron had asked her to contact him.

Chapter 5

Xander had packed a few snacks in his bag, mainly dried nuts and fruit, and offered some to Obie, which she declined. The landscape hadn't changed much, except it was wetter in some spots as the tide completely receded.

Obie had been quiet for the last thirty minutes, which suited him. But he had a feeling it didn't suit her.

She'd been talking and chatting most of the time they'd been walking and while he wouldn't say he knew her, clearly something was up.

"You okay?" he asked. He'd asked her earlier but didn't mind repeating himself.

"No. I mean I know I said yes before but honestly who's okay after a day like we've had?" she said. Then she shook her head, her hands shaking as she tried to push her hair behind her ear. He was used to long endurance hikes from his time in the SAS and hiking up near Mt. Wilson in LA, but she clearly was reaching the end of her rope.

"I'm rambling. Sorry."

He stopped walking and turned to face her. "It's okay. You're okay. Everything you're feeling is normal."

"Nothing's normal," she said under her breath.

He took a gamble on the fact that she wasn't used to being chased or in life-threatening danger. She needed a distraction again. "That's life with Aaron."

"Is it?" she asked. "I know you haven't seen him in ten years but was he always…? How was he?"

God, the one thing he really didn't want to do was unpack the past, but right now that was what she needed. What his client needed, he reminded himself. And talking to her made it easier to keep his temper in check. He was mad at his brother, really pissed at the men who'd shot at them, and it was taking every bit of training he'd had to keep himself in that null zone. The one where emotions had no sway.

It didn't help that Obie was hot as hell. His body was noticing and his mind was tempting him with images of that kiss he'd denied himself earlier. Getting physical with her *would* work to kind of get him to that Zen headspace he needed to keep moving. But sleeping with a client was a big no-no. Not that Van had ever explicitly said it, but Van would never be impersonal with someone he'd hooked up with, would never risk hurting someone purely because of attraction. He just wasn't one of those people who was casual about sex.

Most of the time Xander limited himself to masturbating or some sort of no-strings exchange with one of the few women he felt like he could walk away from.

Obie was already different. This Florida woman with her quiet strength and resilience.

"Xander?"

"Sorry. I'm not going to say it's complicated again

but Aaron, my brothers and I have always been jumbled together. I think that's why I didn't call you back when I got the message. I just needed time to figure out if I was going to come here."

She licked her lips again and his eyes tracked the movement behind the dark lens of his sunglasses. His cock jumped and his skin felt too tight for his body.

His mind was busy listing all the reasons why he couldn't have her, but his body wasn't really paying attention. Instead some part of him was conjuring up images of her naked in his arms, his mouth moving over hers and then down the side of her neck, following the path that a bead of sweat was taking.

He jerked his thoughts away from that.

"Why did you come?" she asked.

He stopped and fumbled in his backpack, very aware that he needed a few moments to get himself back under control. He took a deep breath and pulled out his reusable water bottle, taking a long swallow before offering it to her. Their fingers brushed as she took it and all of the calm he'd forced on his body was gone. His pulse raced as a shiver of sensual awareness went up his arm and then straight to his cock.

She'd asked him something, but for the life of him he couldn't recall what it was. Something about why he was here.

"My boss is big on family. So I tried to weasel out of coming and Van said, 'He's your brother. Go.' And here I am."

"Does Van know your brother?" she asked, handing the water bottle back to him, and this time he was careful not to allow their fingers to touch.

"No. But he knows me. Our team… It feels more like real family than Aaron does to me. But Aaron and my brothers, they were…are a big part of the man I've become and I think… Well, not to get too deep but Van knew I'd regret not coming before I did."

That was one of the things he liked about his boss even if sometimes he resented it. Van always put the team members' best interests at the heart of everything. They worked hard and the job came first, but Van made them all feel as if what they were doing made the world a better place.

They were his found family. It was odd because the Price Security team wasn't like what he'd believed family was growing up. There was no fighting or yelling and everyone just had each other's back. He hadn't known that kind of group existed.

"So here I am," he said. "Sorry I didn't call you. If I had maybe…maybe you'd be safe at your coffee shop instead of in the swamp."

"Maybe."

"Just maybe?"

"Well. The thing is…once I found out that Aaron was involved with La Familia Sanchez cartel I had to find out more."

"Why?"

"It's complicated," she said with a wink at him. But her expression was closed and her mouth had tightened. As much as she was trying to keep things light, she couldn't. It was just a guess, but based on what he'd learned so far, she built her toughness up herself and she didn't want to let him see any cracks.

"Isn't everything?"

"Yeah."

He put the bottle back in his backpack. In a few more kilometers they'd reach the lake and he'd already decided they'd use the inflatable pack-raft he had in his bag to traverse it. They started walking again and she fell into step beside him.

"The cartel?"

"It's not really anything solid. But my dad was the sheriff and was investigating their movements through central Florida when he and my mom were killed."

"And the cartel was suspected?" he asked.

"By me and my brother. But the cops said it was an accident."

That was a lot to unpack. But it wasn't really that uncommon; many cartels and shady organizations had plugs within law enforcement. Corruption happened everywhere. "Why did you think it wasn't?"

Obie blamed the swamp and this wild day for why she was bringing up her parents. But also there had been a hint of honesty in the way Xander opened up about Aaron. Something that she always felt like she had to reciprocate.

Also, if she was being brutally honest with herself, she wanted him to tell her she was grasping at straws, and maybe make her give up on her idea of asking Aaron to find out more about her parents' deaths.

Something that every logical part of her being was sure would lead to nothing.

But her heart was hoping. Her sixteen-year-old self needed answers. Needed to know their deaths were something other than a random accident. Obie truly wanted to believe that her life hadn't changed so drastically, that she'd lost her parents and brother in the span of a year, for something random.

She wanted that loss to have a meaning. At the time grief had been overwhelming, and then with Gator's departure she'd struggled just to survive, but today mired in the swamp she wanted the truth for herself and justice for her parents.

If it didn't reveal anything, if it was just random… Well, she didn't want to dwell on that either.

So why didn't she believe her parents' deaths were an accident? As a kid she'd trusted the cops and didn't want to believe someone who worked for her dad was also in with the cartel. "They died in the swamp. That's the first thing. Daddy grew up in the Green Swamp. And Mama was from Georgia and knew how to survive in the bayou and had learned our swamp as well."

"Were they out walking in it?" he asked.

Though he'd said he was a bodyguard, the way he was asking questions and listening told her that he must have done some investigation in the past. She was so tempted to leave off talking about her parents and steer the conversation back to him. But she wanted answers, and Xander was making her view the situation differently.

"No. They'd taken the airboat."

"It broke down?"

She shook her head. "If it had Daddy would have fixed it. He was always fixing it and knew that airboat like the back of his hand. They hit a tree and the airboat exploded."

He raised both eyebrows, seeming surprised by her revelation. "Having seen your skills behind the wheel of the boat and in the swamp...that does raise a few questions. What did the medical examiner find?"

"The bodies were charred from the fire," she said, her voice cracked as she relived the grief and pain she'd felt back then. She'd never seen the bodies; Deputy Wade had made sure she and Gator hadn't. "They said that Daddy had a heart attack and lost control."

Logical. It was the only explanation that would make sense for two people as savvy about boats and the swamp as her parents had been. But her father had been in excellent health on his previous checkup only a year earlier. Deputy Wade had pushed for further investigations but it had been shut down by someone higher than him. Obie and Gator had believed that Wade was right to ask them to continue and resented the fact that he'd given up so easily.

As an adult, she almost got it. Sometimes in order to keep a job, rules had to be followed. But Wade had been friends with her parents and had been Gator's godfather. In Obie's opinion he never should have stopped looking into it.

"You don't think he did?" Xander asked, pulling her back into the present.

"He was healthy and he'd been close to arresting

someone in the cartel. Daddy believed that someone had been using routes through the swamp to smuggle something. Not being vague but he wasn't sure if it was just drugs or drugs and guns and maybe people. He saw a small hunting hut that looked as if it had been used as a shelter. He cleaned the trash out of it and when he checked in a few days later he could tell someone had been sleeping there again.

"He found the trail of the persons staying there and found some stuff—I'm not sure exactly what—but it made him suspicious and he brought it to his superiors, who told him it was nothing. He and Mama had gone to check it out the night they died."

She hadn't realized how much she'd been holding on to until the words spilled out of her. It had been such a long time since she'd allowed herself to think of them and even longer since she'd spoken of that night.

"So…you think the cartel killed them?" he asked.

She heard the questions in his voice. She had no proof, and even to her own ears it sounded like a string of circumstantial incidents. But she wasn't going to back down from her beliefs. "Yes."

"You think Aaron was involved?" he asked.

She hadn't even considered that. "They died ten years ago."

"Just about the time that Aaron and I lost touch. But I'm not sure that he would have been in the cartel then."

She let out another ragged breath. "I really don't think he's responsible. I just hoped maybe he could get some information for me."

Which sounded impossible to her. Xander seemed as if he wasn't sure what to say and she got that. "Yeah. So that's why I came to Key Largo this afternoon. I don't know what info Aaron has on the cartel or if it's all bullshit to keep himself out of prison, but I thought maybe there's something that will lead to some answers for my parents' deaths. Maybe something to connect the cartel to the deaths of other sheriffs. I'm not really sure what I want to find."

She'd never been sure if the cops had shut down her and Gator's concerns because they knew her dad's death had been the key to something bigger and more dangerous. In her heart she knew her parents would never have been involved in anything shady. But he could have been a target for trying to stop it.

"You want answers," he said.

"I do."

"I get that. I'm not sure what Aaron knows but I can ask my boss to look into it."

She appreciated him saying that and figured he was just being nice until she looked up and their eyes met. He was sincere. His blue gaze held hers. He put his hand on her shoulder and she knew he had her back. It had been a long time since she'd talked about this and even longer since she'd thought someone would be at her side. "Okay."

"So I guess even if I'd shown up we might still have met," he said.

"Probably. Would you have seen the threat before they shot at us?"

He shrugged. "Who knows? I mean I saw you enter and I was watching the house and didn't notice them."

"Should you have?"

"Maybe. I think I was in my head. Aaron and I have a lot of history. I mostly hate being told what to do. I didn't want to be ordered to come to Miami."

"I'd be pissed if my boss forced me to do anything," she said. But Helen wouldn't have had to force Obie to go if Gator called. In fact if Obie as much as heard a rumor about her brother she would follow it. "But I would drop everything if Gator reached out. Family is blood, and you don't go against blood."

Obie would do whatever she could to help her family. There was a well of caring inside of her that was obvious. She'd handled everything the day had thrown at her but her emotions were clearly deep given the way she talked about them.

Part of Xander wanted to open up to her. He wasn't that guy. Never had been. That was his secret shame. He just couldn't feel the things that others did. Instead of feeling empathy when someone was devastated, he got angry and enraged. Not helpful, as his mom had pointed more than once.

At Price Security there were protocols in place that made it so he didn't fail. There were always backups. Right now he'd give his right arm to have his best friend, Kenji Wada, by his side. Kenji saw things that Xander didn't but he was also very good with people. He could do the small-talk stuff that Xander didn't want to.

But Kenji wasn't here.

Xander had never felt more like he was failing than he did at this moment. Meanwhile Obie watched him in that quiet way of hers. What was she trying to find in him?

Probably some reassurance that he'd keep her alive. She'd been shot at and forced to go deeper into the swamp and it was clear she wasn't prepared for this. She'd brought up the cartel. He really didn't know anything about them but sent the information to Lee so she could pull up everything the internet and dark web had on them.

"I know you would do anything for your family," he said at last. "But I'm not that guy."

"Why not?" she asked.

He started to shrug but she just sort of rolled her eyes. "Don't lie. It's okay to just not answer."

As empathetic as she was, it didn't translate to her being a pushover. She'd probably shared more than she'd meant to about her parents' deaths and now she wanted to even things up. At least, that was his guess.

"I didn't make you tell me about your parents," he pointed out.

"Did I say you had? Listen, we are stuck in the swamp for the rest of the day at the very least and someone is after the both of us. I probably shouldn't have overshared and the conversation sort of naturally went to your relationship with Aaron. I didn't ask any deep, probing questions. You're the one throwing up barriers and acting defensive. I don't know you or Aaron well enough to be judgy about your relationship. That's all coming from you."

He rocked back on his heels. He felt so seen right now. He didn't at all blame her for what she'd said. "Truce."

"Sorry, I just am not someone who is going to be all like sorry you are getting into your feelings. That's not who I am."

Steel ran through her. Why he was surprised was beyond him. He'd seen flashes of it at the house and then in the boat and when she'd been so cool with the croc. Some of the people he'd worked with in dangerous situations would have lost it when confronted with a predatory animal. No amount of training could make someone immune to fear.

"How'd you know how to deal with the croc?"

"I like animals. In another life I might have been a marine biologist. I still like them so I spend a lot of time reading books on the ecosystem of the different swamps and have been studying the Everglades and surrounding areas for the last few years. There are a lot of dangers in the swamp."

"Do you miss living in the swamp?" he asked. He was piecing together the woman before him. She had been so polished and very much like all the women he'd seen in Key Largo and before that in Miami when he'd flown in. She had looked urbane and sophisticated. Now sweat had dissolved her makeup, leaving her skin fresh and tanned looking. Her hair had lost that board straightness, curling and escaping the ponytail holder she'd caught it up in.

She seemed at home here. Learning about her upbringing in the swamp helped it make sense. But why had she left and changed so much? And having done so, why was she still keeping her knowledge of the swamp? Plus if she was talking then she wasn't asking him uncomfortable questions.

"I didn't think so," she said. "Should we get going?"

"Yes. When we get to Cuthbert Lake I'll inflate the pack-raft. I think it will be easy to cross and quicker than walking all the way around it," he said.

"You have a pack-raft?"

"Yeah. I mean it's Aaron so I sort of prepared for everything," he said.

"What's everything?"

"Land, water and air escape," he said.

"Air?" she asked, eyeing his huge backpack with its 120-liter-capacity tag on full display. "Really?"

"I'd call Van for a chopper if needed."

"And we don't need one now?"

"It's for emergency use only. It's expensive and involves a lot of paperwork," he said.

"So are you some sort of British Boy Scout? Do the Brits even have Boy Scouts?" she asked.

"Yeah. But I wasn't one. I simply do better when I have a plan for every outcome," he said. Some things he knew couldn't be anticipated. His brother's accident, for one thing. Aaron sending his hot coffee shop boss into a dangerous situation for another.

Reacting to her like he was.

He still wanted her. And no matter what he did to distract himself, she reeled him back in.

It made his skin feel too hot and his concentration harder to hold. But it was the truth. He was pretty damned sure that was a truth she wasn't looking to hear from him.

But he couldn't deny it or ignore it any longer.

Ah, hell.

He didn't want to tell her the truth about himself because he didn't want to disappoint her. And women never really reacted well to a guy saying hey, I don't do feelings but let's hook up. Or at least not a woman like Obie, with her big brown eyes full of unspoken feelings, staring right into his core.

Chapter 6

The mangroves they'd ditched the boat near gave way to a saltwater swamp that would lead them to the Everglades, about a couple of days' walk to the northwest. The swamp was different from the one she'd grown up in but she'd come to love these southern swamp areas. The mud flats and sand were thinly covered by seawater during high tide, but because the tide was out, it was just wet as they walked across it.

Most of the plants that thrived in the area were able to tolerate tidal flooding, such as their saviors the mangrove trees, which grew and formed thickets of roots and branches. Their thin, tall roots anchored them to the sand. Providing the perfect cover for Obie and Xander as they moved farther away from Madeira Bay.

She smiled as she noticed some crabs and other shellfish feeding on the fallen leaves and other materials from the decaying roots of the mangroves. She loved seeing this side of nature. And though she limited herself to visits to the Miami Seaquariam these days, she missed being in the water and the swamp, the feeling of being at home.

Birds flew overhead circling and looking for their

lunch, making Obie aware that she hadn't put any snacks in her purse before heading out to Aaron's house. She hadn't been prepared for any of this. Which was probably a good thing. Who wanted to be prepared to be attacked by a vengeful drug cartel, right?

"I had no idea the swamp would be so...alive," Xander said.

"Marine biologists call this area the nursery of the ocean because so many species thrive here and come here to spawn. Fish who lay their eggs in the salt marshes ensure their young have plenty of food and some protection in the swamp grass as they grow," she said. She'd spent a lot of time reading up on the swamp. As much as Aunt Karen wanted her to forget, a part of her had never been able to.

"I can see why. In my head I was thinking of the bayou in Louisiana when I thought of the swamp. But this area isn't what I was expecting," he admitted.

"Florida usually isn't," she said. "I mean my Florida. Not the theme parks or condos on the beaches but the quiet, natural Florida."

"You live in the swamp?"

She shook her head. She didn't want to get into the messier parts of her past. But being here again, feeling her hair adapt to the humidity and the heat wrapping around her in a comforting way reminded her of being with her parents before they'd died.

They moved farther inland, and while the ground wasn't as wet it also wasn't totally dry. The swamp was a dense ecosystem that sort of worked as a filter between the sea and the land. And the land in Florida was very porous. She wanted to take a moment to dig her feet into the sand like she had as a girl. But she knew her swamp reunion wasn't really a happy one.

They had a lead on the men following them, but eventually their pursuers would find their discarded boat and be on their trail again.

"Which direction should we go?"

"We need to get to Cuthbert Lake," he said. "I have the coordinates in the map on my satellite phone so I can check it in a few minutes but if we stick to heading west, northwest for now we should be good."

She trusted him. She had no choice. Her phone had Google Maps but wasn't really getting much of a signal out here. Plus, when she mentally listed her skills, the ones she had didn't come close to his. He'd literally shot a man who was trying to kill her.

Obie focused, watching the swamp creatures and birds flying overhead, trying as much as she could to pretend this was a normal day. But the swamp had ceased being normal to her a long time ago. The time away created a much needed distance, but also some uncertainty if she could survive there again. Being chased by gun-toting thugs wasn't helping either. "Tell me about your team."

"What do you want to know?" he asked.

She glanced back over her shoulder at him. "Well, is it a big team? You mentioned Lee and Van."

"There are six of us. Van's the leader. He put the team together and once he recruits you to work for him… Well, he says we're family and I guess we are. We all live in a condo tower in LA that Price owns when we aren't out on assignment."

That sounded…interesting. Was that the right word? It was unconventional to say the least. "Why?"

He rubbed the back of his neck and looked down at his watch. She glanced over at it and saw a compass on it, but she was pretty sure he'd done that to distract himself rather than check for their direction.

"Not sure. We all work a lot so the apartments are a nice perk. It doesn't make sense to own a home when I'm on the road most of the time."

"Sounds like my place. It's not really home but just more a place to crash."

"Why is that?"

Now it was her turn to look for a distraction. "Just is. So the rest of the team?"

"Not letting that go, are you?"

"It's a long walk to Cuthbert Lake, figured we might as well chat more," she said.

"Fair enough. You can tell me about your coworkers at the coffee shop, deal?"

"Deal," she said.

Her coworkers were fun and funky and made the job she took after college seem like it wasn't really her giving up on her dreams. But she knew in her heart she'd gotten her degree in hospitality management to please Aunt Karen. A part of her still regretted not following her own path and going into marine biology.

At the time she'd thought the only life for her had been the one that she could copy from the other people around her. She'd been afraid to let herself continue to be a part of the world she'd left behind, even if it caused problems. To her there had only been the new life in Miami or her old life as a swamp girl, no in between.

Aaron had unintentionally given her a new perspective with this adventure.

Maybe she could have both.

His team. He missed them. If Kenji were here he'd be miserable in the heat but probably wouldn't show it, sticking to his slim-fitting black suits and dark glasses. His Japanese American friend wore his glossy black hair long in the front with a huge fall of bangs and short in the back. Kenji was lethal with any weapon, but then all of the team were. It was the trust they'd developed as friends that made them such good partners in missions like these.

"I'm probably closest to Kenji. He's damned smart and lethal. We spar a lot. Then there's Rick. He used to be a DEA agent and frankly would probably be better in this terrain than I am. He's really good at blending in and finding paths out of any situations. Then there's Luna. She looks kind of unassuming, but she's fast and smart and puts things together faster than the rest of us. Lee is sort of tactical and stays in the tower— that's the offices and apartment building. She keeps us all connected to each other, she's going in the field more often now. Her skills are legendary. She used to be with a secret government agency. So she tends to give very little away."

Obie stopped walking, turning her face up to the

sun and watching a seagull flying overhead. "I like the sound of your team and that you listed their skills."

He glanced at her. Was she teasing him?

He was pretty sure she was. But he still wasn't used to it, being treated like he's not too scary to joke with. He'd been this big and bulky since birth. His mother told him to smile and people would think he was friendly, but based on his last attempt with Obie it clearly wasn't so easy.

Somehow his early-childhood memories, the positive ones, had been obscured by that one horrific teenage incident. Sixteen had changed him and made him into the mess he'd been when Van found him. He had read enough psychology books to know that he'd grown past that experience and he'd made peace with his part in the accident. Something that had been a long time coming.

But he hadn't been able to forgive Aaron for his part. Was he holding on to that lack of forgiveness because he knew that it had been chance that Aaron knocked their brother Tony to the ground where he'd hit his neck on a rock and taken the spinal cord injury that had paralyzed him? Xander could easily have done the same thing to their other brother, Abe, or even Aaron. It could have been *any* of them, but it had been Aaron and Tony, all because Tony asked a girl out that Aaron liked.

So juvenile. And the impact of that day changed them all forever.

"You okay?"

"What?"

"You look scary and angry."

He shook his head and closed his eyes. Of course he did. Thinking about the past always brought him back to the man he used to be. "Sorry."

"Was it the teasing?" she asked. "I was just trying to make things feel a bit more…normal."

"I liked it," he said. "Keep doing that."

"Do you work with your team often? You mentioned you were closest to Kenji."

He remembered the first time they'd met. Neither of them was keen on being on a team. Kenji was so polished and Xander had sort of hulked into the room in sweats and a plain T-shirt. On the outside they were complete opposites, but when they hit the mat to spar it was clear they were two sides of the same coin.

Over the years they'd grown closer and Xander had learned a lot from Kenji through playing games, sparring and observing his way with others.

"We don't always work together but there are times when the entire team is needed for a job. We all have a different skill set."

"Do you prefer working on your own or with the team?" she asked as they continued walking toward the lake.

"Both," he said. "It's nice to be a part of a group on assignment but I can't do it all the time."

She nodded her head. "Same. I like when my entire crew is in the coffee shop during the rush and we are all doing our part but then I need some alone time and usually escape to my office and close the door."

"You seem pretty outgoing so I wouldn't have thought that."

"I can be. I mean I do like being around people most of the time. But after the rush we all need a break. Aaron was good about making everyone laugh. He seemed like such a nice guy…not saying he isn't but learning he was dealing was a shock."

What had led his brother into the drug cartel? Being booted from the SAS changed him, and it changed Aaron as well. His brother had been in the wind for longer than anyone in the family liked to acknowledge. Part of the reason why he'd been reluctant to come and see Aaron. Their mom had tried several times to reach Aaron but she never got in touch.

Perhaps what he was doing for a living had kept him away. Xander wanted to believe that was the case. That his brother had been trying to protect them all. But there was another part of him that wasn't entirely sure.

Maybe Aaron completely separated himself from the family because he no longer felt anything for them.

Xander wasn't going to get any answers until they were out of the swamp and he had a chance to talk to Aaron. He was definitely going to discover the truth—not just for their family, but also for Obie, who Aaron shouldn't have used.

The things she liked about the swamp were coming back to her, but she didn't necessarily love all of it. She'd learned to live under Aunt Karen's roof and found things to appreciate there. The swamp girl she'd been had no real place in the life that Obie had carved for herself.

Working with other people and enjoying being around them was all a product of her life with Aunt Karen. She'd been encouraged to socialize. Aunt Karen even signed Obie up for all sorts of clubs in high school and they had helped to transform her.

Aunt Karen had done the same thing for Gator but her brother just hadn't settled into it. He didn't want to be on the baseball team or in the math club, even though he was really good at both. He'd just wanted to be back in the swamp. Back home, he'd said.

But home for Obie had been tainted by their parents' deaths and the questions around it. Home was a distant memory and not a place. It had become something inside of herself. And if Gator had been able to stay with her at Aunt Karen's she might have been happier in her new life.

After Gator had left, she'd had a fight with Aunt Karen and it had taken Obie about a day to regret not going with him. So she'd swiped Aunt Karen's debit card and gotten enough cash for a bus ticket back to Winter Haven.

Dumb.

So she skipped school the next day and went to the bus station, which had scared her. She'd only ever been in her small town near the swamp or in the suburbs with Aunt Karen. The bus station had been in the city and it had been frightening.

She'd almost turned back but she knew if she had even the smallest chance of catching up to Gator she'd have to get to Winter Haven and then get a ride out to their home between Lake Alfred and Haines City and then get in the swamp and search.

The bus ride had been long and she'd deliberately turned her cell phone off so she wouldn't have to lie if Aunt Karen called. She'd pretended to read a book on the bus so that the person sitting next to her wouldn't talk to her. She'd had her iPod and her headphones in the entire time listening to Green Day because they'd been her mom's favorite band and trying not to cry.

She'd hated that feeling and never wanted to experience anything like it again. When she got off the bus in Winter Haven she had been shocked to see Aunt Karen waiting. The older woman was pale and her hands were shaking.

She gave Obie a lecture but then told her to get into the car and they'd drive out to her parents' old place. At the time Obie had been pissed that one of her cousins might have ratted her out, but now she appreciated that Aunt Karen had been worried about her and the fact that she'd taken her to the house had meant a lot.

Gator hadn't been there. In fact, no one had been at the place in months. Aunt Karen had been trying to sell it so Obie and Gator would have the money to pay for college. Eventually the house did sell and Aunt Karen gave Obie the leftover money after paying for her community college courses.

She shook her head. Why was she thinking about the past? Why was the swamp showing her not the perfection of her childhood but a greater understanding of what brought her here as an adult? Maybe the truth of her life was somewhere between the swamp girl she was deep inside and the sleek urbanite that her aunt had helped her become.

As much as she felt she was forced to change, another part of her knew she had wanted to. At least a little.

She saw a snake slithering toward them, jerking her away from her thoughts, and she put her hand on Xander's arm to stop him. They watched the colorful snake until it slithered past them.

"I can never tell the king snake from the coral snake," Xander said.

"That was a king snake," she said. "They are bigger than the coral and of course not poisonous. The color pattern is so similar. I had to wait until it was closer. The king snake's red and black bands touch each other. Coral always touches yellow."

"I think I'll just keep trying to avoid them both."

"Good idea," she said. "I'm pretty much that way with everything in the swamp. Most creatures are dangerous if pushed but if you let them be you're okay."

"Aren't we all?" he asked.

She thought he might be teasing her now. "Some of us more so than others. Why do you think those men tried to kill us?"

"It's easier than taking you hostage and killing you later. They can just search the bodies, find the information they are looking for and dump the bodies. Now that they aren't sure if we've read the SD card and/or contacted anyone, they will probably try to take us alive."

Great. "Do you think they'll stop if we get rid of the card?"

"No."

She stopped walking and put her hands on her hips as she shook her head at him. "You could at least pretend to think about it. Give me a little bit of hope that I can stop them from following me by doing something."

"Yeah, I'm not like that. The truth is until that information is used in some way they aren't going to stop coming after you. I know that's not easy to hear but that's the truth."

She had suspected that was the situation they were in. "And you think your team and Crispin can help?"

He didn't answer, which wasn't reassuring. As much as she'd have wished for some platitudes, his silence told her what she needed to know. He wasn't sure if anyone could help them. Which meant they had to escape with their lives on their own. And even if she got out this time, the next…

She dropped her arms and turned to start walking again but he stopped her with his hand on her shoulder.

"I'm not leaving your side until you're safe. That's my promise to you," he said.

Gratitude washed over her. He was a stranger still, despite what they'd been through together. But she knew that he'd keep her safe. That was one thing she was sure of in this day where nothing seemed right anymore.

The moment Aaron had been arrested, normality had gone out the window. Her life was swirling around her and she felt like that scared sixteen-year-old again.

But this wasn't the start of something else. This was some weird in-between thing that, at this moment, Obie couldn't see a way out of. She wanted to tell him that she appreciated having him by her side but he was the reason she was here. If he'd come to Miami when she'd first called, maybe she wouldn't have had to go to Key Largo.

But then she wouldn't have known that Aaron was connected to La Familia Sanchez cartel. She wouldn't have this chance to maybe find out what had actually happened to her parents and if the cartel had been involved. That chance at closure was too tempting to keep her away from Xander. She needed to see where his investigation led.

It wasn't exactly a fair trade-off. Her safety for answers about her parents. Answers she wasn't sure she'd ever really get.

"You okay?" he asked.

"No. I'm not okay. There is a part of me that feels like this is going to go on forever and I'm not getting out of the swamp or out of survival mode. And I left that behind a long time ago. I don't want to be back in that situation."

"We will get out of this. In fact when we get to the marina at West Lake I'll have my team take you to a safe house. I can set a trap for the cartel and get to the bottom of Aaron's involvement with them."

"Flush them out? How?"

"I'll set a trap," he said.

"I'd like to help with that."

"Uh, no way. You're a civilian and you need to stay safe," he said.

She hated it when someone told her what to do. She knew she wasn't trained like he was. He had a point, but if he was staying in the Everglades then he needed her expertise. "Would you set a trap in the swamp?"

"Yes," he said.

"Then you need me. I'm your best chance at catching them and not getting killed or injured in the process."

"I need you?"

"Yes."

Chapter 7

"Someone's coming," Xander said, drawing Obie off the rough path toward the surrounding marshier area. Lush vegetation and brackish water deepened as they moved toward the large cypress trees with their knobbly roots.

Not exactly an ideal place to hide.

Obie grabbed his wrist and pointed toward the mangroves, which were thicker and lower to the ground, providing more coverage.

He nudged her to go first and then followed her as she sank back into the water as it deepened and found a way to get under the branches of the mangrove tree, using their tangled roots as shelter.

His pack was large and didn't enable him the maneuvering that Obie had done. She mimed taking his pack off and held her hand out to him. He handed it to her and she pulled the waterproof hiking sack toward her, shoving it under the water and dragging it into the shelter she'd found. He ducked into it just as the first person came into their view.

Two men wearing Army green utility pants and matching T-shirts appeared. They had on dark sunglasses and from their build Xander guessed they had to be security of some kind.

He noticed that they had on shoulder holsters and both men had earpieces in. They looked like military and he waited to see what they were going to do next. Had Van sent the military to find them? Seemed unlikely since Van knew that Xander would get the two of them to safety, and more players could sabotage their mission.

One of them put his hand to his ear and then spoke in Spanish, which Xander didn't speak so he couldn't understand.

He glanced at Obie, who shrugged, which he took to mean she didn't understand them either.

They spoke quickly but he heard the words "gringos" and "Quentin."

Making a logical assumption, he was pretty sure they were working with the cartel. But these guys were in a different league than the men he and Obie had encountered at the house in Key Largo. These guys were trained to track them down through difficult terrain. Only someone with knowledge of this area would be able to keep finding them so quickly. If he ruled out military they'd have to be mercenaries. And so far he'd seen no indication that there were any government agencies involved in this.

Which begged the question what the hell was on that SD card of Aaron's that had the cartel sending guys like this after them?

He knew he was going to have to get the card from Obie at some point and read it.

As they moved closer, Xander leaned toward Obie

and whispered in her ear, "Try to form a good impression of the men so we can give their description to the authorities."

She nodded; her face was very serious as she turned back to look at them. They stayed still and Xander concentrated on the men, and not the snake they'd seen a few minutes earlier, or the crocodiles in these waters. Right now the threat from humans was the only one he could focus on.

The men were both tall, but the left one was slightly taller. Both had identical tattoos on their arms.

Maybe a cartel symbol?

He took particular attention to those details, which he'd relay to Van and the team for further research.

The person closest to them seemed uneasy and kept watching the path in front of them more than looking in the vegetation. But the other one was carefully skimming each of the bushes and roots of the trees. Xander pulled his knife from his belt—his gun was in the sack and useless once it got wet. He was confident he could take both men by hand if he needed to.

As they got closer, he took a deep breath and coiled his body so that he was ready to attack. Obie touched his shoulder and he ignored her. He was in fight-and-protect mode. Whatever she had to say could wait.

She squeezed; he tilted his head toward her so she could speak into his ear but didn't take his eyes from the men, who had stopped walking.

She leaned in, but then didn't speak, as the men were now looking toward their hiding place.

He hand tightened again, but he heard her hold her

breath and knew it was fear and not trying to communicate with him that had caused the squeeze. Something moved out of the water in front of them. A small American crocodile, probably about four feet long. Perhaps their friend from earlier. The men froze and the crocodile ambled past them into the marshy area and then into the water near the mangroves on the other side of the path.

Both of the men waited until it was gone and then started walking farther down the path. Once they were out of sight Obie let go of his shoulder. "I was going to warn you about the croc."

"Thanks. The men were the bigger threat," he said, pushing his knife back into the sheath. "Do you think we're safe here for a few more minutes?"

"I don't know. The croc sort of swam up while we were waiting. The swamp is a living ecosystem."

"I know that. I just want to let them put more space between us," he said.

"Do you think they know where we're heading?"

He had no real idea. It was concerning that their stalkers came from the direction of the marina they were trying to get to. But it was a day or so hike from here, and there were two lakes they had to cross before they got to it.

"We'll stick to the mangrove swamp until we can't," he said. "I'm going to have to rely on you to watch the swamp and I'll watch the path."

"I can do that. Do you want your gun?"

"Yes. But I have to keep it dry," he said. "Right now it's better in the sack. I can handle a few guys with just a knife."

"I'm glad to hear that," she said, but there was a ragged note to her voice.

He wasn't sure how much more she could take before she reached her breaking point.

Obie searched for the calmness she'd once had in the swamp, but it had been a long time since she'd had rely on her skills for survival, and back then it had been just a game between her and Gator. Other than that one scary bus ride and a few times she'd walked alone to her car in a dimly lit parking lot, she hadn't really had to rely on her own skills. She also wasn't a fan of staying in the low water while the tide was out, but then when it started to come in she didn't prefer the rising water encroaching on her either.

She focused on it though. She didn't want to let her mind wander to the two scary guys who'd been looking for her and Xander. She begrudgingly reminded herself that Aunt Karen might have been right when she'd encouraged Obie to take Spanish in high school and college. Not that those lessons had been helpful at all when listening to the two men talking. She hadn't really understood anything.

They'd looked scary, and that had been about where her mind had settled. Her heart raced, and then she'd felt the current in the water stir around her and saw the croc. She'd almost let herself panic before recognizing that panicking was going to get her killed either by man or beast.

Xander was a calming presence at least. He was just so *big*, and there was something reassuring in that. She remembered the way he'd looked when he'd tackled her to the floor at Aaron's house, and every moment after that when he'd kept her alive. A stranger, but one that she was coming to rely on.

She knew her limits and what she was capable of. But Xander had skills that she'd never considered acquiring, and maybe it was time to sign up for kickboxing or some martial arts class at the strip mall where her coffee shop was.

Though a part of her thought that might have the same real-world applications as the Spanish she'd taken in college. Which wasn't reassuring considering how little she had understood from the cartel members.

Her mind was starting to wind into a place where anxiety would take control. She had to find something else to think about. Really she wanted to keep talking. Just open her mouth and let all the wild thoughts and fears in her head out. But talking would give them away.

She also didn't know if those two guys were the only ones looking for them.

Xander was close behind her. He'd taken his pack and put it back on, and he wore his sunglasses again as the sun was bright. The water reflected the rays back into their faces.

She was *hot*, and even though she tanned easily, she could feel her shoulders getting sunburned. She wished she'd put on the linen button-down she'd left in her car before running in to check out Aaron's place. But she hadn't. Hadn't known where all of this would go. She was stuck with what she was wearing.

Again her anxiety started to tug at her. She closed her eyes and stopped walking. Just took some deep breaths and did box breathing to calm herself. Xander stopped.

"What is it?"

"Just need to catch my breath," she said.

He put his hand on her shoulder, his thumb rubbing against the side of her neck in a very comforting and reassuring pattern. Her breathing settled and his touch teased her. Her mind thought about him standing behind her. If she closed her eyes she could almost—almost!—pretend he was a guy she'd met in a sweaty club and maybe they were pressed together waiting for drinks.

Except the tide was rising around her feet, almost up to her calves, and a crab scuttled over her foot.

Yeah, this wasn't the distraction she wanted it to be.

"Thanks," she said.

"Want me to go first?" he asked. "Are you worried about what's ahead of us?"

She felt some laughter welling up inside of her and swallowed it because she recognized it as more of the same panic she was trying to manage. "I'm just scared."

"You'd be foolish if you weren't. That's perfectly normal."

"Are you scared?"

"I'm cautious," he said. "I don't know the terrain so that worries me, but those men back there don't bother me at all. I've fought men like them all of my adult life. So if they worry you, you can relax on that front."

She shook her head. "Everything is bothering me. I

can't shut my mind off and I know I need to stay quiet but here I am talking to you."

"I'm glad you are talking to me. What's one thing that you are concerned about?"

"If there are more men looking for us," she said.

"I'm sure they are moving in a grid pattern and the two we saw are the only ones in this area right now. We might move into the next part of the grid they are searching and encounter different people."

"What will we do?"

"What we did last time, and if they spot us I will take them down," he said.

There was so much confidence in him. This entire thing was outside of her comfort zone, but he was settled into it. More at ease here in the swamp with men chasing them than he had been in the boat as they'd crossed Madeira Bay.

This was what he did; he'd said that to her. But her mind hadn't been able to comprehend what being a bodyguard meant until this moment. He was in his element putting himself in danger and keeping her safe.

She appreciated it more than she thought she would. Knowing that he was with her was all the reassurance she needed. He'd asked her to keep an eye out for swamp dangers and she couldn't let him down. Wouldn't let him down.

After an hour they hadn't seen anyone else on the trail. It seemed they were alone for now. Which suited him. The tide had been steadily rising and was up to his thighs, almost to Obie's waist. "Let's move back on higher ground."

It had been a long time since he'd had to survive in the outdoors. He forgot how much he hated wet socks and shoes. As soon as they were on the trail he wanted to ditch them, but the path looked rough, and Obie was walking it in a pair of flip-flops. He wasn't sure he wanted to chance it.

Her legs looked long and lean under the hem of her shorts and she took a moment to wipe her hands down them. "I always feel so odd when I'm half-soaking-wet."

"Does it happen that often?"

"No, thank goodness. But I was tossed into my friend's pool on Memorial Day weekend and managed to only get the bottom half of my body wet."

It was odd to hear about her life outside of Aaron and the coffee shop. He didn't have a complete picture of her despite her talkative nature, and maybe that hadn't mattered when they were initially staying still around snakes and other swamp creatures.

But now it did.

They were relying on each other to survive, and neither could do it without the other, but there was more to it than that. He liked her. He could no longer deny that fact. He wanted to know her better. For the first time he felt comfortable opening up to someone and he was already wondering if he'd be able to see her after this was over.

"The last time I experienced anything close to this was SAS training. We were on a three-day survival hike on Snowdon in Wales. Hated it then, not really loving it now."

She smiled and it went straight to his groin. She was pretty when she relaxed and wasn't worrying. Not that she wasn't pretty at the other times, but a stressed-out woman needed comforting, not lust.

"So a survival hike… You signed up for that, right?" she asked. "Sort of seems like you might have been to blame for your experience."

"Too right. Aaron signed up first and so then I had to because I wanted to prove I could do anything he could."

"Are you older or younger?"

"Younger by eighteen months."

"That explains it. And you both made it to the end?"

"We sure did. I got there first but only by a few minutes," Xander said. That boy-man he'd been seemed like a different person to who he was today. Back then, winning and proving he was the faster and strongest had been the most important thing. He hoped he'd changed.

But honestly, he wasn't sure.

His line of work was different. There was no competing in bodyguarding. His objective was keeping his client safe and alive. So he had a lot of wins in that case. But there were also days when he needed to win in a real situation, not just keeping a client safe. That's when he and Kenji sparred hard. Kenji liked to win as well.

"Were you close growing up or was it always a rivalry?" she asked in that innocent way that people did when they learned he had a sibling so close in age.

His childhood was two parts, before and after the tragedy. But the young years… "Yeah, we were close with Abe and Tony as well. But we were always fighting to be the alpha. Abe is four years older than me and then Tony is three. They always had the jump on us because of that, but that just made me hungrier to one-up him."

"Did you ever succeed?"

Yeah. But he didn't like to remember that moment. Or what came after. "Not really. I figured out that type of winning isn't satisfying. Now that we are out of the water I want to try to sync the map again and make sure we are still on course."

"Okay."

He pulled his phone out and saw they'd drifted a little bit east on the last part of the trek. So he made an adjustment to the direction they were heading. "Did you see that tattoo on their arms?"

"There were a lot of them," she said. "I could only see the one closest to us."

Xander opened the drawing app on his phone and used his finger to make a rough sketch of the tattoo he was talking about. It was a snake wearing a three-pointed crown.

"I've seen that before."

She was pale and her hand had gone to her mouth. "Where?"

"On Aaron," she said. "Do you think he told those men to come and find us?"

From jail and the holding cell he was in, Aaron wouldn't be able to do that. All of the doubts he'd been trying to create, to tell himself his brother wasn't in the cartel, were gone. "I'm not sure. I don't believe Aaron would send you into a trap. Okay, so that tattoo might be for the cartel. I'm going to send it to my team so they can research it. Do you remember any other details?"

"Well the one on Aaron is on his left forearm and it has the letters in a Latin script under it. The letters are *LFS.*"

La Familia Sanchez. That made sense. This connection was confirming that his brother had taken a dark path after they'd both left England.

He was the younger brother but he had always been the one to look out for Aaron, who was smaller than him. Was this his fault? Everything since Tony's accident had taken them on a path that Xander wouldn't have believed possible when they'd been boys. Whatever information they found on that SD card was probably going to show him a picture of his brother that he didn't want to know.

One question remained in Xander's mind right now. Was his brother so much a cartel man that he would send an innocent woman to her death to retrieve information for him? Because there was no way Aaron hadn't known the task he'd given Obie was dangerous. That was why he'd called Xander first.

Chapter 8

Her phone pinged as Xander was inflating the pack-raft. She pulled it from the drybag. A message from Crispin Tallman, the assistant district attorney. She unlocked her phone and started to call him back.

Xander still wanted to wait for his team before they called the cops. She knew he was right that they needed someone to facilitate turning themselves in, but at the same time, not calling the cops seemed wrong. Maybe the DA could help.

Xander said they were persons of interest in the shoot-out at Aaron's, which of course she knew they'd been involved in. In her entire life she'd never broken the law or committed a crime. She was a stickler about those things.

"What are you doing?" Xander asked.

"I'm fixing to call the district attorney. He left a message for me," Obie said.

Xander walked over to her and she was struck again by what a big man he was. She stood there for a moment, the phone in her hand. "Let's hear the message."

"Sure," she said.

She dialed her voice mail and put it on speaker.

"Ms. Keller, I heard there was some trouble at Aaron's house. Are you okay? The cops said there was gunfire. Call me and let me know you are okay, please."

She smiled. "I think he can help us with the cops. I'll call him and let him know what happened."

Xander crossed his arms over his chest. "How well do you know the assistant district attorney?"

"Just met him today before going to the house on Key Largo. Why?"

"Just trying to get as much intel as we can. Okay, call him but keep it on speaker."

"Why?"

"Only my brother and this guy knew you were going to Key Largo," he pointed out. "Aaron's in jail and asked you to get the SD card, so only one other person knew you were going to be there."

"The man who is trying to cut a deal with your brother and to get some hard evidence against the cartel," she said. "He's on our side."

"He might be. My job is to keep you alive and I don't know him."

"Are you always this…?"

"Thorough? Yes."

"I was going to say paranoid," she said smartly. Her dad had been a cop, and as a result Obie always trusted law enforcement and government officials. That didn't mean they were always right—after all, she still wasn't sure Officer Wade had acted in their best interests, but it was hard for her to believe that Crispin would have set her up. He'd seemed to want the information that

Aaron had for himself. Obie was one sure way of him getting it, wasn't she?

"Call it whatever you want. Until I talk to him I won't know."

"He said his men had already searched the house and found nothing," she pointed out. "He was skeptical I'd find anything."

"But still encouraged you to go," he said.

"Stop that." But his words made a certain sense. She just couldn't imagine someone from the district attorney's office would have been involved in that incident at the house. "I trust him."

"Then let's call him," Xander said. "I'm new to the situation. All I had before I landed was your name and Aaron's. We have no idea who the men were who shot at us. They could have been waiting for an associate of Aaron's to show up and you triggered them when you did."

"Associate? Does that mean they think I work for him?"

He shrugged. "Who knows. More likely they think you're his girlfriend."

Obie felt her anxiety flaring up and she wanted to just throw the phone and the SD card in the water and turn and walk deeper into the swamp, until she was completely cut off from everyone and everything. She was tired of this.

She wanted to go back to her old life. As much as she'd felt like she was playing a part working in the coffee shop and going back to her apartment every night, at least she knew what to expect. Not like this. Where everything felt out of control.

Xander put his hand on her shoulder and squeezed. "Sorry. I shouldn't have been grilling you. It's my job to keep you safe and to do that I act like everyone else is a threat. Doesn't mean they are."

"Why is it your job?"

"Because I didn't call you back," he said. "If I had maybe you wouldn't have come to Key Largo."

Maybe.

She licked her lips, which felt like they were getting sunburned, and then hit Crispin's number. The phone rang three times before going to voice mail. She looked over at Xander, who just sort of nodded at her. She took that to mean she should leave a message.

"It's Obie Keller. Wanted to let you know I'm okay. I'm with Aaron's brother and we are trying to get to a marina. Men followed us from Aaron's house."

Xander tapped her shoulder and made a cut-it-off motion.

"I'll try to call again later. Bye."

She hung up and glared at him.

"What?"

She could tell he wanted to say something else about not trusting Crispin but instead he just looked at his watch. "It's getting later and I want to get to the marina so we can get out of here."

"Me too," she admitted. As soon as she could, she was going to give the SD card to the assistant district attorney. She wanted this entire thing far behind her. Talking to Xander about her parents' deaths and saying out loud the things her sixteen-year-old self had believed made her realize that she would probably never find the answers she wanted.

And if it meant not getting shot at she'd be okay with that.

"Hey, would you humor me and do something?" Xander asked.

"What?"

"Take the SIM card out of your phone. I know you trust the man you called but your phone can be traced. Someone might have a tap on his phone," Xander said. "Until we know that the cartel didn't follow you there I think it would be the safest option."

She didn't mind doing that and handed her phone to him. He removed the SIM card and returned both to her. She put them back in the drybag with the SD card.

"Let's go."

Xander had to wonder if he was just getting too paranoid or not. Obie's reaction to his suspicion of the district attorney's office wasn't out of line. Of course since it was Aaron who'd sent them into this mess, Xander's objectivity was shot. Nothing had gone right since the moment he'd seen Obie enter Aaron's house.

He pushed the pack-raft into the water and held it steady while Obie got in. It was a two-seater, which was a necessity with his six-five and two-hundred-fifty-pound frame. He normally needed the extra space. They both fit, but it was tight. She was sitting between his spread legs, her back against his chest.

She shifted around to get the oars, her butt rubbing

against his groin, and he once again remembered that moment he'd been trying so damned hard to forget. That millisecond when he'd let his control slip and almost kissed her.

He stared down at the top of her head and then the back of her neck. A bead of sweat was there, slowly inching its way toward the fabric of her tank top, and he inwardly groaned. Then realized he'd made the noise out loud when she turned to look over her shoulder.

"Sorry if you're cramped. Let me try to shift forward and give you more room."

She put her hand on his thigh, lifting herself up, and her hips rubbed against him. He started to harden and put his hands on her waist. "You're fine. Just stay still."

His voice was gruff and harsh to his own ears. But she settled back against him…and he noticed the moment she felt his erection against her back. Her posture went stiff as she realized she'd turned him on. "Sorry."

"Stop apologizing. I'm sorry I can't help my body's reaction," he said.

She just took the oar he'd given her. "Okay. Tell me when to row."

He did, and as they moved farther into the water and found a rhythm, he was able to uncover some calmness. His body got used to the feeling of her against him, and he was able to rein in the thread of sensual awareness that had slipped from his grasp. He'd never struggled to control himself before, especially when he was working, but Obie had somehow gotten under his skin.

"Can we trust your people?" she asked after about ten minutes had passed.

"Yes. Why do you ask?"

She kept rowing. "You said only Aaron and Crispin knew I'd be there, but your people knew you'd be there."

She had a point and he almost smiled at the way she was analyzing the situation. "You're right. But they sent me to help Aaron and wouldn't have sent gunmen to prevent me from leaving."

"Are you sure? You're bossy," she said with a note of teasing to it.

"I am. But they know that about me."

"Were you particularly annoying before you left?"

"Surlier but that's my MO when I'm not working," he said dryly. "We can keep that as a possibility but I'm putting Price Security at the bottom of the threat list."

Price Security wasn't just his workplace; they were a family and they were way too close for there to be a mole in the organization. But he respected Obie for not ruling anyone out. He liked the way her mind worked.

"Who's at the top?"

"I'm not sure. I'll have a better idea after we talk to Lee later but I think the cartel have someone on the inside. It's not too farfetched to think they have someone in jail who keeps them informed."

"To that point, they know Aaron was arrested and might have been watching his place."

He had thought of that possibility after she'd defended the assistant district attorney. Probably because of how he was, Xander tended to always think that anyone not at his side was against him. Time and time again that had been proved true, and as much as he didn't want Aaron to be a potential accomplice, Xander knew he couldn't rule him out. Yet. "That's probably how they found us. Sorry if I sounded—"

"As you said it's your job to keep us alive. I think everyone is a suspect until we can rule them out," she said.

"Agreed."

She rowed a bit more. "Alligator to the left."

He glanced over at the object he thought was a piece of wood and then realized it was a gator sunning itself on the top of the water. "I thought gators and crocs weren't in the same ecosystem."

She tipped her head to the side and he could see her smiling. "The Everglades is unique and has a diverse landscape. Gators stick to the fresh water. American crocodiles are mainly in coastal area and rivers. They prefer salty water and tend to congregate in brackish lakes, mangroves and the like. The American crocodile is the only species other than the saltwater crocodile to thrive in saltwater. They are always fighting for survival down here and their population is monitored because of development and the degradation of their habitat."

When she talked about Florida, there was affection in her voice. There was a beauty to her when she forgot to be whoever it was she wanted him to see and just relaxed. She seemed at home here in this wild part of Florida. She tipped her head back up toward the sun and the breeze stirred around them as she continued to row.

She was in her element here. He knew what had made her leave. But he wondered if she regretted it, and if this errand that she'd gone on to help a friend would make her want to return.

There were so many questions he wanted to ask her. But given his body's reaction to her earlier he kept silent.

He felt on edge and irritated not just at the situation but at his past and his brother. He hated that they were in a place where he had to rely on the woman he was trying to protect. He did better when he was the one in charge—and the one to blame.

Obie wasn't used to keeping people safe, not in this type of situation. She deserved him at this best, but she was getting a man who was too busy trying to keep his emotions in check.

Xander knew that was one thing he tended to fail at. Damn Aaron. Why hadn't he stayed clean and kept Obie out of this?

He needed a distraction. Not Obie talking about the swamp or her curvy hips pressed against his groin. He needed someone to come out of the dense tree coverage on the lake, armed and ready. He needed the kind of threat he could observe and then face and defeat.

Xander fascinated her. He had clearly been turned on by her but he kept a tight leash on himself. She had to be honest—there was a part of her that wanted to push him and see what it would take for him to let go. She knew he wanted her the way she desired him. He'd almost kissed her and then of course there was his surprise boner, but he wasn't doing anything sexual when they were alone.

He also kept their conversations bland. Safe. He wasn't one to give anything away, so it had been nice when she'd gotten a reaction from him when she'd called him bossy. Aunt Karen wouldn't approve of her behavior, poking a man who wanted to keep his peace. But for the first time in years that didn't matter.

The deeper they got into this wild, untamed land, the more she felt the old Obie returning. She had shut away her memories of living in the swamp because they'd been too painful. Hearing the cicadas singing in the heat of the late afternoon made her remember the feel of the hot gray sand of the swamp under her bare feet, until she dug into it with her toes and felt that cool wet layer lying just below.

Florida was complex, both savage and beautiful at her heart. The cities had clawed out their existence along the coast and paved over so much making roads and malls and restaurants on the rest. But the real Florida couldn't be tamed or kept at bay forever. The bugs and the gators and the verdant trees and bushes that grew wild and out of control were constantly fighting to reclaim the land.

As she rowed across the lake seeing snakes and gators swim past them, she accepted that the savage beauty of the swamp was starting to reclaim her as well. When she'd left the swamp she'd been lost and damaged. What child could lose their parents and not be? And the only way to survive at Aunt Karen's house was to become more like her. That was the way to a place she'd found she could enjoy some peace.

It was also a cop-out. That was probably what Gator

had been saying when he claimed that he no longer recognized her. He had been trying to tell her that she was hiding from who she truly was.

But that girl…that swamp girl who was more at home in bare feet and cutoff shorts had no place in Aunt Karen's gated subdivision or her fancy private school.

She hadn't missed that girl. That girl had been sad and scared and angry. Shedding her had been the only way that Obie had been able to survive. But after a decade she was ready to look back at her past with some maturity and maybe…figure out a way to be the woman she'd always thought she would be.

She heard the low rumble of thunder and looked up, realizing that storm clouds were gathering behind them as the wind started to pick up. They were halfway across the lake. Damn. There wasn't really a chance of them making it across before the storm got to them.

"We need to find shelter. I think we can make it to the shoreline over there," she said, pointing to the right.

Xander glanced behind them, saw the blackening sky and nodded. "Let's do it."

For the first time in a while she felt Xander's strength as he dug deeper with each stroke of the oar and propelled the boat forward faster than before. Her strokes weren't really helping anymore and she took her oar out of the water. He could move them more quickly without her.

The first fat raindrops hit them as they got close enough to land that they could step out of the pack-raft and pull it to shore. He got out and lifted her out behind him, he handed her his pack and her shoulder bag while she waded to shore, then maneuvered the pack-raft behind her.

She scanned the trees at the shoreline and moved farther into the dense swamp area. There wasn't going to be any real shelter but if she could find a tree with some large branches… Except lightning was still a threat. She stopped and waited for Xander.

"I'm not sure what's safest. Rain is a pain but can't kill us, lightning can so I don't want to be too close to a tree," she said.

"Good idea. Just move us away from the lake. Maybe some of those mangroves that are lower to the ground. I have a tarp we can use to protect ourselves if you want to stay in the middle of the path."

She looked around. It had been a long time and she had been a girl the last time she'd been outside in this kind of storm. With her daddy and Gator. They'd found shelter together on a log and Daddy had used his big rain slicker to keep them dry.

She looked around and saw a spot that would work. She pointed to it and Xander moved with her. They sat down on the log, which was lower than the trees and shrubs around them. He lifted the pack-raft up over their heads and used his pack on one side and a bush on the other keep it suspended over them.

The rain increased, falling hard on the bottom of the pack-raft. Thunder rolled and they saw cracks of lightning as the storm grew in intensity, raging around them. Xander put his arm around her as the wind increased and water blew up under their makeshift shelter.

She leaned into him, stealing a bit of his warmth as she shivered. She looked up to check on him and make sure he was okay. He was smiling as the storm raged. And then he looked down at her. His eyes met hers.

She put her hand on the side of his face and smiled back at him. There was something about being alive while this wild storm cascaded around them. She shifted and leaned up until her lips brushed his and he opened his mouth, taking the kiss that she'd been craving.

Chapter 9

The rain was heavy, drowning out all the sounds around them, and her mouth was warm on his under the intimate shelter of the pack-raft. The kind of heat that he didn't mind. For the first time since he'd seen her pull under the carport at Aaron's house, he relaxed. Her mouth was firm and she tasted so damned good.

He didn't kiss many women on the mouth, and he tried not to let this be special but it undeniably was. She had kissed him. He probably wanted it more than she did.

In the past, he wouldn't have allowed himself to have this. Partially because he had rarely felt anything like this before and partially because he was on the job. But this wasn't a regular job anymore, no matter that he'd told her it was. He was here for a very personal reason and it was hard to keep those lines from blurring. Harder than he'd realized it would be when he'd first grabbed her in his arms and run with her earlier that day.

He put his hand on her shoulder. She was small but strong; he'd seen her strength enough to know it would be foolish to underestimate her. But she was still in over her head.

His mind was trying to keep processing and making a contingency plan, but her tongue rubbed against his and every base instinct he possessed roared to life. He put his hand on the small of her back and drew her closer to him as he deepened the kiss.

He felt the brush of her fingers against his neck as she held his face with just that one hand. Her mouth opened under his and she seemed to lean the slightest bit closer to him. The world outside the pack-raft had disappeared. It was all rain and thunder and lightning.

She lifted her head and he felt the brush of her breath against his lips. She licked hers and his body sort of clenched everywhere.

"If I was out of line, I'm sorry," she said.

He didn't know how to respond to that. He was pretty sure she was teasing him but he wasn't usually jokey with women. Maybe that was why he didn't have many women friends… Lee and Luna were sort of friends, more like family. And they weren't Obie. He had no freaking idea how to handle this.

"Technically I'm not being paid to protect you so I guess it's okay," he said.

Immediately, he knew he'd said the wrong thing.

She pulled back, wrapping her arms around her waist, canting her body away from his. "Glad to hear that."

"Hell, Obie. I suck at this. Want to know why Aaron I aren't close? We don't do relationships. We do fighting and one-upmanship and proving ourselves but we don't talk and sometimes there are things that need to be said. And as you've just witnessed I suck at saying the right thing."

She looked back at him. Taking in all he'd said. "That's a lot to drop on a girl. First of all, did you want to kiss me?"

"Hell yeah, I did. I know that I need to stay focused to keep you safe," he admitted. "I promised I wouldn't let anything happen to you."

Her arms dropped from her waist and she swiveled slightly back toward him. "Do you always keep your promises?"

"Definitely."

"You're a very serious man. But Aaron isn't despite how similar you say you are."

"I know. We all deal with life in different ways."

"Fair enough. My aunt does it through her rules," she said.

He assumed that comment was meant for herself and not really for him. "How do you do it? Deal with life without losing it?"

"By pretending to be someone who fits in. It's easier if you are just like everyone else. For a few moments it seems like you belong," she said. "You?"

The raw honesty in her once again struck him. How did he deal? "Rules like your aunt, I guess."

"Why?" she asked. She pulled her knees up to her chest. It was still pouring down rain but not as heavily as it had been.

"It's safer that way."

She reached up and took the ponytail holder out of her hair, running her fingers through it. "Safer how?"

How to explain without revealing how out of control he always was. Van said that part of Xander's strength was that he had all of that fear and rage inside of him and that he channeled it. But Xander wasn't channeling it at all. He'd caged it inside of him. Occasionally something escaped, and it enabled him to be ruthless when he protected his clients.

But it always felt like he was one moment away from a nuclear meltdown. From everything being shot to hell. From him ruining everything again.

She looked over at him, her eyes clear and seemingly safe.

"I'm one big rage ball inside. Rules are the thing that keep me in check," he said.

She tipped her head to the side. The humidity made her hair shorter and curlier, and one of the curls fell over her forehead. He reached out and pushed it back behind her ear like he'd seen her do earlier. Any excuse to touch her because now that he'd kissed her, he wasn't going to be satisfied until he had her under him or over him.

In his arms, naked, both of them taking and giving everything they had.

But how did that fit into the rules he'd made for himself?

It didn't.

"I don't see that," she said. "You've been calm under pressure and haven't hulked out one time."

"I'm at my best when I have to get someone out of danger," he said. "Bullets and bad guys fit into my rules for the world. I know how to dodge and outmaneuver them."

"What doesn't fit, then?" she asked.

"You."

"Oh." She gave him a sad smile then. "That kiss didn't mean I want to be with you forever."

"Maybe not to you. But to me…"

What was he going to say? That he craved her more than anyone he'd met before. He knew forever didn't exist, not the way she probably meant it. Marriage. Family. Those were words he had always felt weren't for him. But when he kissed her, he tasted something that made him crave a different life. One where he was a different man who might be able to fit into a family and have what he'd denied himself for so long.

Why had she kissed him? That was the main question running through her head as the rain started to lessen. And what the heck had he meant?

This day was stirring up too much baggage that she would have preferred to keep hidden for the rest of her life.

She'd been shot at, which wasn't helping things, and kissing him had almost made it so she didn't have to keep reliving that moment she'd been yanked from Xander's arms. The intent on his face had been intense and she had no doubt that man would have killed and then searched her dead body for Aaron's SD card.

Maybe she should focus on that instead of on the kiss she'd taken from Xander and his oblique statement.

"What do you think is on the SD card?" she asked.

"My guess either drop houses or names of people

in the organization. Whatever it is… Well, seems like Aaron has something important in the right hands to stop the cartel and hamper their operation," Xander said.

"Do you think we could read it? I mean they are going to kill us whether we know what's on it or not."

"They definitely are going to try but I'm not going to let them succeed," he said.

Once they were talking about the men chasing them and the SD card, Xander fell into a sense of calmness that hadn't been there when he'd been kissing her. Which was a good thing, right? She wanted this man to be hot and bothered by her.

She just also needed the capable version of him to make sure they got out of the swamp alive. Then take down the cartel and help her find out if there was any connection to her parents' deaths.

But it made her want to know more about him, to see him after this chaos was done. She hadn't been making small talk when she mentioned Xander's personality was very different from his brother's. Aaron was always flirting and chattering and making everyone laugh. There was a temporary quality that Xander didn't possess.

Xander was solid and sure of himself—oh, Aaron had confidence but it was draped behind his carefree image. With Xander's build and the way he held himself with that military stance, tall, shoulders back—nothing was getting through him.

Was that why she'd kissed him? Why she couldn't get him out of her head?

"You will put up a fight and that is reassuring. What do you think about reading the card?" she asked.

Trying to force the conversation back on the card since that was the safest thing for her at the moment. She started to laugh and realized that exhaustion and the stress of the day was getting to her. She laughed until she started to cry and the tears did that screwed-up thing of turning from mirth to fear in a moment. Then she was for real sobbing and pushed herself out from under the pack-raft, standing in the pouring rain so maybe he wouldn't notice.

Yeah, right.

Like this was any better. But at least she wasn't under the pack-raft anymore contemplating how knowing the details of a drug cartel's operation was the safest option for her at the moment.

She wrapped her arms around her waist and then felt Xander next to her. He didn't say a word, just pulled her into his body. Those big muscly arms of his wrapping around her. She put her face into his chest as she kept crying. He didn't say a word, just held her and honestly that was the only thing she could have handled at this moment.

Slowly the tears stopped and she knew she should step back but he smelled good, sort of a mix between expensive cologne and man. Like him. The other guys she'd dated and had sex with over the last few years all smelled of the same generic, artificial Prada cologne. Xander smelled and felt real.

Like swamp real. Not sophisticated Miami real.

In her head that made sense.

* * *

The rawness of Obie's tears was hard to shake. She'd moved on in a way that he appreciated, admired. Accepting her feelings, then focusing on the task at hand. He had always felt like his anger set him apart from everyone else, but without saying a word Obie had shown him that they weren't that different despite the unique emotional storms they had weathered.

He checked the map and for messages from Lee. There weren't any new ones but that didn't surprise him. She wouldn't send word unless she had news.

He let her know the name of the assistant district attorney that Obie had talked to and suggested she coordinate with him in their teams messaging service. She thumbs-upped it.

"Lee is going to reach out to that assistant district attorney and let him know what's going on," Xander said.

"Thanks. Could she also let my boss at the coffee shop know I won't be stopping by later?" Obie asked.

He relayed that information for her and synched the map coordinates to his smart watch and put his phone back in his drybag. Obie wore her pack and had his slung over her left shoulder.

As she stood there, no sign of the tears or the fear that had been present earlier, his body stirred again. It was hard not to be impressed by her resilience. Everyone had a core of inner strength whether they realized it or not.

"Ready?"

"Of course," she said. Her stomach rumbled as she

said it and she looked a bit embarrassed as she put her hand over it. "Sorry, I'm used to eating a bunch of little meals during the day."

"Totally cool. I do that too. I have two protein bars—want one?" he asked.

She handed him his pack and he opened it, finding the bars and tossing one to her. She took it, opening it carefully. "Thanks for this. I'm pretty good at fishing. But we'd have to build a fire and hopefully we won't be in the swamp for that long."

"Hopefully. But if we are I have a camp stove," he said. "According to the map it's about another two hours to the marina where we are going to try to check in with the team. If I know Van he'll have transport waiting for us."

"Van's your boss?"

"Yeah," he said, shouldering his own pack before lifting the pack-raft. Obie took the oars as they started walking. He followed the trail they'd taken to the shelter and she fell into step beside him.

"You like him?" she asked. "You talk about him and Lee like they are family."

She wasn't wrong; they were family to him. Probably the only people who knew the man he'd become, and Van in particular was very aware of Xander's past, having bailed him out of jail after a drunken fight that had left another man in the hospital. Van, with his angel-wings tattoo on the back of his neck and his intense calmness, had come to visit him in jail.

"He offered me a chance to change my life. Told me if I wanted to learn to control the rage that I kept directing out to the world then he'd show me. Or I could spend the rest of my life getting locked up for fights until I took it too far and ended up in prison for killing someone."

Telling her about his past wasn't what he intended. He should be focused on the task at hand. But he had realized when he'd held her in the rain that nothing with Obie was as he intended.

"Wow. How did you do that? Because I'm not going to lie, you don't seem like the kind of man who would do those things," she said.

He thought about the last ten years. None of it had been easy. He started doing other things rather than fighting. He worked out twice a day, and the assignments that Van gave him at Price Security were usually physically demanding. Even the ones that weren't required a lot of concentration. Van kept him busy and Xander had found that by using his mind to solve puzzles, his hands to repair things or to play chess against Kenji—who probably could be grand master if he put his mind to it—helped him a lot.

He just always kept *busy*. That was probably why he was talking to her. There was a lot of downtime in the swamp as they were making their way through it.

But both of them were still on high alert, Obie listening for deadly creatures, him on the lookout for gun-toting cartel members. Their skills were keeping them one step ahead of danger.

The danger he couldn't avoid came from the woman she was. Adept at adapting to this environment, showing him her strength and intelligence and he wanted her. He had to keep talking about the stuff that he didn't normally address because it helped to put up a barrier between them in his mind. A barrier that he was going to use for as long as he could to keep from reaching out and pulling her back into his arms.

"I am that man. I've just learned how to control myself."

That was a hard thing to admit. He had been trained by the British military and his fighting instincts… Well, he'd been born with them, but the military had honed them. He'd never thought about reining any of that in until Van. Van had shown him that his true strength didn't come from hitting as hard as he could or his endurance. It came from marrying his mind and his body together. Something that he was really leaning into on this trek through the swamp with Obie.

Chapter 10

The fact that Aaron wasn't the man she thought he was had been driven home so many times today that she wasn't sure why having another acknowledgment of his connection to the cartel was giving her chills. He'd told her he had intel on them, asked her to go and retrieve it. But a part of her had been hoping he wasn't as involved as he must be to have that tattoo. It frightened her that her instincts, which she'd always prided herself on, had been so wrong.

"Are you okay?"

"Yeah," she said because talking smack about his brother wasn't going to make her feel better. The person she was really disappointed in was herself. Why did she let first impressions sway her? But she had and beating herself up about it now wasn't going to help.

Xander sent the rough sketch he'd drawn as well as a description of both of the men to his team and then shut his phone down, putting it back in his drybag. "We are a bit off course so we need to head more to the west to get back on track."

He acted so normal about this. Seeing men with guns searching for him was just an everyday thing.

Was there any way she could tap into his attitude and maybe make it her own? Maybe find a way to just be chill. Like, *Yeah, guys with guns are tracking me but I'm cool.*

Not in this lifetime.

She longed to be back at her little apartment right now, getting ready to go in and do some unpaid work ordering supplies or double-checking the receipts for the last week. Anything mundane and away from the swamp and the two Quentin brothers.

Xander was doing his level best to keep her calm and be reassuring. But she didn't know him well enough to relinquish her power like that. Probably even less than she'd known Aaron, who'd worked at the coffee shop for over a month.

But now she doubted that. She hadn't known Aaron at all. She'd seen something in him that had reminded her of Gator and blindly thought he was the same as her brother. Someone who needed her help.

Someone she didn't want to let down.

Someone who'd led her into a world she'd never thought to return to.

"I've never really liked coffee. I mean give me a lot of sugar and some cream and then I can tolerate it but not coffee on its own," Xander said.

The comment was so out of left field it threw her for a second. She looked over at him and saw a hint of concern on his face. He was trying to give her something else to think of other than the gang tattoo that had been on Aaron's arm.

And it was definitely *just* Aaron's tattoo and not the two men who'd been tracking her that bothered her.

Coffee?

He wanted to talk about *coffee*?

She was half-tempted to give in to the manic panic that was trying to dominate in her mind, but she shook her head hard. "I love it. I think it's because my mama used to give it to me and Gator when we were little."

"With sugar?"

"Oh, yeah. You'd have loved it. She served it to us in these demitasse mugs that had been her grandmother's. She'd put in a big teaspoon of sugar and fill the mug halfway with milk and then add in the coffee. Each morning we'd sit on the back porch watching the swamp come to life, drinking our coffees with her and she'd tell us tales of the swamp."

In her mind she saw her mama with the thick brown hair they shared, curling around her head as she talked in that deep Southern accent of hers. Some mornings they'd been chatty; other mornings the swamp had been. The animals and birds who woke up and started moving about. They'd just enjoyed being present, something she'd forgotten in the last decade.

"Do you still drink it that way?"

"No. Once I moved to my aunt Karen's I stopped having sugar. She also wasn't a fan of dairy products like milk and cheese. Too many calories."

"I need as many calories as I can get. I burn a lot," he said.

"I imagine you do." She couldn't help glancing over at him, trying to be surreptitious as she let her gaze move over his big, muscular body. She liked his large biceps and really appreciated his strength. His body was a testament to his own ability to survive.

"So now you take it black?"

He kept distracting her and in that moment she thought she really liked this guy. This man who'd shown up out of nowhere and now was saddled with keeping her safe. He could have just been stoic, dragging her along behind him through the swamp, but he was aware of her next to him. She felt seen by him in a way that made her feel unique, special and safe.

"Yes. Though sometimes Hilda, who owns the coffee shop, comes in and makes this Cuban coffee. It's really strong espresso and she puts in condensed milk. Oh my God, it's so sweet and strong. It's delicious. You might like it. Lots of calories."

"You can make it for me when we get out of here," he said.

"Will we?" The words just slipped out. In the back of her mind, she didn't see that happening. The last time she'd been in the swamp her parents had died. It was almost as if she was afraid that…she might not make it out either.

Sure, they were walking and he had his satellite phone, but the truth was that the men following them were dangerous, and no matter how many nice distractions Xander offered her, she was scared and unsure.

It was nice having him by her side, but that didn't mean he'd be able to save her. The only sure thing was herself.

The rain started to lessen and she moved to step back but he held her. "Just a minute longer."

She stayed there, putting her own arms around his middle and hugging him back. He had been honest to a point about Aaron, but coming to help his brother out and finding himself on the run with a strange woman had to be jarring even to a man like Xander, who was used to protecting people.

Was he protecting people because he couldn't protect himself, or had he failed to protect someone else?

The rain nearly stopped and she stepped back from his embrace again. This time he let her go. "We should get back on the water if we are going to make the meeting point before dark."

"Affirmative," he said.

She smiled. He went full-on protector mode after he let his mask fall and his emotions were present. "I'll get the packs again."

"I want to check the map and I'll grab the pack-raft after that. I think I might have something to read the SD card in my bag. Lee always has a tech pouch she insists I carry."

His voice softened when he talked about the members of his team in a way it didn't when he talked about Aaron. She got it; she felt the same way about her family at the coffee shop. They all cared about each other, and it was so much easier than her relationship with her blood relatives. Aunt Karen was still demanding and Gator…he was in the wind. But she couldn't help hoping that maybe this would bring them back together.

* * *

Xander wasn't the best at small talk, and coffee had been the only thing he could think of to discuss. He wasn't entirely sure it had been helpful, but Obie wasn't as pale under her tan as she had been since the moment he'd drawn that tattoo on his phone. She had history with the cartel, and his brother hadn't exactly been forthcoming with all that his "favor" from her would entail.

He was tempted to ask Van to get her out of the situation so he could go hunting and find a man they could get information from. Except that course of action was a slippery path that he hadn't allowed himself to get back on in a long time.

It would be easy to blame his brother for the rage that was building inside of him. He was very tempted to just forget the training and the past ten years of the man he'd become and go back into eliminating any threat.

If he'd been alone, he might have killed one of the two men following them on sight and then pressed the other one for information. He didn't like to harm anyone, but sometimes that was the only option if it meant rescuing others, and if it came down to keeping Obie safe he'd do whatever was necessary. A part of him regretted that he hadn't done it even with Obie here. But then maybe the fear in her eyes would be directed at him and not at the cartel.

That shouldn't matter. Most of the time Xander didn't really give a crap what anyone thought of him. But somehow he wanted Obie to see the best side of him. The noble bodyguard. The brother who was some-how better…hah. He wasn't better than Aaron. He just had gotten lucky when Van had found him and offered him this job.

He had to remind himself that.

The Quentin boys were dangerous, and that hadn't changed just because they'd all left home and hadn't been in the same spot for too many years. They were still a threat to anyone who crossed them.

"You are getting out of this, Obie Keller," he prom-ised. "Don't doubt it. And when you do I hope you'll make me that coffee."

"If—"

"When."

"Sure I'll make it for you. But Hilda's is better. She also makes the best black beans and rice. Have you had that?"

"No, I don't think I have," he said. "I have had beans on toast. One of my favorites."

"Gross."

"Excuse me? I think I'm offended by that," he said. She seemed lighter now and he'd do anything to keep her from drifting back to that scared spot she'd been in a short while back.

"I'm offended by beans on toast… Actually what is it?"

He laughed. "It's what it sounds like. Toast and then you open a can of Heinz baked beans and put it on the toast."

"Heinz? I thought they were catsup people."

"Over here maybe but in the UK they have the best beans."

"Hmm… When we get back to Miami you can make it for me."

He looked over at her, saw that she watched the trail in front of them, occasionally glancing back to check and see if they were being followed. "Deal."

They walked in silence for another twenty minutes before she stopped. "I need a break. And maybe a moment alone."

He suspected she might need the toilet. He did too. He looked around and then back at her. "Do you see a spot that would be safe for us to use?"

She took a moment to walk along the marshy mangroves and then nodded. "Over there should be safe."

"Okay, go first, I'll keep watch."

She didn't hesitate as she moved into the underbrush and behind some trees and bushes. He shrugged out of his pack and took out his Glock 22 handgun. Unless things went wrong, they should be able to stay on the dry part of the path until they reached the lake. He checked his weapon, and the clip he had in it before putting on the safety.

Obie came back and smiled at him until she noticed the weapon in his hand. "What's that for?"

"You. I figured you'd feel safer with it while I dash into the bushes."

"I don't know how to shoot a handgun. My dad had a rifle to scare snakes and other critters away but it's been years since I've used it."

He gave her a quick lesson. "The safety is on. So

you'll have to flip this switch before you fire. If you hear someone other than me, take the safety off. Those men we saw earlier will kill you."

Her hand shook as she took the Glock 22 from him. But she looked determined. "Does it kick? Should I use two hands?"

"If you want to you can," he said, showing her how to hold the gun with two hands and how to aim. "I doubt you'll have to use it but better safe than sorry."

"Yeah. Okay go fast," she said.

"I will," he reassured her. He dashed into the underbrush where she'd gone and quickly did his business.

He hurried back to where she waited. She handed the gun back to him as soon as he was within arm's reach. "I'm glad you're back."

"Me too," he said.

Her hair now framed her face now in a riot of curls instead of the smooth strands she'd had when he'd first seen her in Aaron's house. The swamp was changing them both. It was clawing away at Xander's controlled facade, and it was changing Obie from the urbanite she'd been in Key Largo to this woman who seemed to belong here.

Holding a gun wasn't her favorite thing, but she appreciated that he'd thought to try to make her feel safe. Honestly she wasn't as scared as she'd been earlier. There was something about Xander…he radiated an assuredness that she hadn't allowed herself to feel in a long time.

"That sounds good. Do you have anything to cook with in there?"

She'd seen quite a few crabs. And in the briny water, clams flourished. She could gather some stuff while he inflated the boat.

"I have a small camp stove."

"Great. I'll get some fresh seafood and we can cook it in the salt water. That way we can eat. I'm getting hungry."

"Me too," he admitted. "I do have some more protein bars as well."

"Good to know." Of course he did. He seemed to have thought of everything.

They continued walking and she glanced over at him. "Does anything surprise you?"

"You did," he said. "I mean I knew you'd called but I assumed that once I didn't call back that would be the end of things for you with Aaron."

"I'm not that kind of person," she said. She wasn't. She couldn't just walk away from anyone. That's probably why she was still hoping to find some sign of her brother and the truth about what had happened to her parents. But she also kept in touch with everyone she'd met in college and considered a friend.

Maybe it was because of how alone she'd been after Gator left. Sure, she'd had her new life, but she'd missed having someone to talk to. Someone sort of like Xander, who had just made silly conversation about coffee to distract her from the reality of the situation. She needed that.

She thought maybe everyone did. For herself she

needed people not interactions on social media. She stayed after her shift was over at the coffee shop and talked to Bea or Hilda or whoever had the next shift.

"No, you're not. You really care about Aaron? I mean…was there anything…?"

"Anything…?" *Oh.* He wanted to know if they'd hooked up or were dating.

"No. He was too into himself, doing his own thing. And he worked for me too. I mean that's just asking for trouble when you date a coworker."

"Yeah, today there are all kinds of rules about that," he said. It was clear the idea of her dating Aaron bothered him—but she couldn't help but tease it out a bit more.

"Even if there weren't rules, it's awkward AF if you date someone and then it doesn't work out. That happened to me in at my first job. We were both working at McDonald's and it was fun at first but then after we broke up, I hated when we had the same shift."

Even as a teen, dating had felt like a minefield. She was expected to act a certain way, talk a certain way… and then the few men she'd let into her life broke her trust anyway.

"When was this?"

"High school. So maybe there was some of that teenage angst going on too. I mean Rand was a bit of a player and dated everyone who worked there. So it wasn't him, it was me. I hated that I hadn't realized he was just dating his way through the restaurant."

"I'd hate it too," Xander said.

"Sure, you would. You don't seem like the type of person that would happen to," she said.

"You're right. But that's because I really don't date," he said.

"Why not?"

"The job mostly. My assignments are usually for a few months to a year. That's a long time to be away from a partner. And I also am not really good at opening up. I have heard from more than one of my exes that I suck at sharing my feelings."

She laughed. "I have the opposite problem, or did. Like you I haven't been dating a lot lately."

"Not because of your job, right?"

"No. Just me. In my twenties I was like, never say never. I can change a guy to be a man I want to spend more time with. But once I turned thirty I was like, maybe saying never to some losers isn't a bad idea."

He laughed, making her smile. Aunt Karen had been pushing her to find a trust-fund guy to get engaged to from her social circle, and she'd dated a few, but it was hard work. She had to look a certain way. Dress all preppy and go to the club on the weekends. It had taken a lot of time and she had been twisting herself more and more into someone she didn't really like. Finally she'd said no. Told Aunt Karen she was going to be single until she was eighty and stopped dating.

She had to like herself alone before she was going to be able to like herself in a relationship.

"So now you say never."

"Hell, yes. In fact if Aaron asks for another favor it's going to be a never again from me."

He nodded and smiled, making his eyes crinkle and his face relax. She wished she could stop noticing how good-looking he was. Maybe it was just the fact that he'd saved her from being killed that made him so attractive. Whatever it was, it didn't feel that shallow or simple, and that might be scarier than the situation they were both in.

Chapter 11

"I'm not sure we're going to make it to the marina before nightfall. I don't know the terrain like you do," he said. "Should we try to cross West Lake in the dark or find shelter and do it tomorrow?" He'd heard nothing from Van or Lee, which worried him. Was this situation even more untenable than it seemed?

More than once he'd seen Obie look behind them in fear. There was no way she was going to feel safe until the SD card was handed over to the district attorney's office and the men following them were arrested. He wanted that too. But it seemed like it wasn't going to happen soon.

"Probably find shelter while there's still some light. We should try to get up if we can. I had a cousin who got bit by a moccasin when he was sleeping on the ground. Do you have something we can use as a shelter in your pack?"

"I do. I have a critter- and element-proof tent," he said. "We can both fit in it."

It would be tight, and after that kiss under the raft he wasn't sure that sleeping close to her was a good idea, but there weren't a lot of options.

Hell, something kept biting him and it was swelter-ing hot even as the sun started to set. He hadn't felt like this ever before, unsure of the terrain and what awaited them. There was no way out of the swamp unless some-one was in a body bag. And if they weren't careful, that someone would be one—or both—of them.

But that wasn't a scenario he'd ever accept.

He was relying on Obie, in a way that he normally only did with the Price Security team.

"Good. I saw some larger cypress trees, which would provide some cover but the roots are in water, so they might not hold both of our weights. Or we can go further away from the lake where the trees are a little stronger. We'd also have less threat from the snakes."

"Away," he said. "Let me deflate the raft first."

"Okay. Can I check in with the district attorney's office?"

"I'd rather we wait to hear from my team."

She turned away from him without another word, walking to the edge of the forest area to find a path or trying not to curse him.

He rolled up the pack-raft and returned it to his backpack before following her. "I'm not trying to be controlling. I just don't know what we are dealing with. You saw the gang sign same as me. Logically it makes no sense for Aaron to have sent them. The only other people who knew you'd be there was the district at-torney's office."

"And your team."

"My team didn't know about Aaron's house. They knew Miami and if Van wanted me dead he wouldn't send me to Miami to kill me," Xander pointed out. He was hanging on to his temper by a thread.

Now she was making him feel like he was being unreasonable even though logic clearly showed he wasn't.

"Why do I have to just trust your people?"

"You don't. I am the one who trusts them. If you want to call the district attorney then do it. We'll see what happens."

"You're being an asshole."

"I'm trying to keep you alive and I'm sorry but taking a risk that we don't have to makes no sense. I'm hot, bug bites are now covering my legs and I feel damp in every part of my body. So if you want to call do it. I don't really think I'm going to be getting a lot of sleep tonight so staying awake to see if the men we saw earlier come back is fine."

She shook her head. "Sorry. I'm short-tempered too. I'm hungry and scared and you've been great but I still don't know you."

"I get it." He truly did. He looked around. There wasn't anyone else around as far as he could see. "Why don't you gather some seafood?"

"We're too far inland for the crabs now. We could try fishing but we don't have any bait."

"Protein bars it is," he said. He was feeling like they needed to be moving more quickly through the swamp but there was no way that the two of them on foot could. "Sorry."

"The bars are fine. They will definitely give us some energy."

"Not for that. For being a jerk. I know you are worried too and want to get help. I just… I have a hard time trusting anyone I don't know."

She gave him a slight smile, something she did more and more frequently. "I get it. But you should try trusting me."

"I do," he said. She had no idea how much he was relying on her because she was the expert. She was the only way they were safely making it across this marshy land and to the relative safety of the marina on the other side of West Lake.

"As much as I do you."

He arched both eyebrows. "How much is that?"

"A lot," she said. "Should we start walking around the lake?"

"Yeah. We'll have to find a place to pitch the tent. I have a feeling like everything else in the swamp its not going to be as easy as finding a safe place to put the tent for the night."

"I'm starting to feel a bit like Katniss did in the *Hunger Games*."

"Does this feel like that to you?"

"Yes. I feel like I was ripped from my world and dropped into this survival fest and I don't like it. But hearing that out loud I sound like a brat. I'm just tired like you."

"It's okay to complain," he said.

"Yeah, but you're not."

"Uh, I think I had a meltdown a few minutes ago," he pointed out.

"You were hangry. And I get it. You were thrown into this too."

He was, but he had been prepared for it in a way that Obie hadn't been. She had no idea what kind of trouble Aaron always brought with him.

It was nice to see a more human side to her bodyguard. He'd seemed unflappable when they were being shot at or hiding from crocs and cartel gunmen in the swamp. So she'd been a bit surprised to hear about the heat and bugs bothering him. But it was nice to see that he was more than some kind of sexy, hot robot guard that just kept functioning no matter what.

The protein bars were okay as fuel, but they were almost out of water and had been rationing it. She wished they'd captured some of the rainwater to drink. Not that it was totally clean but it would be better than lake water. She'd always thought of herself as a survivor but suddenly that was taking on a different kind of meaning. This kind of survival was pushing her to her limits and stirring fears that she hadn't realized she'd hung on to.

At first it had been sort of fun being in the swamp. Down by the coast with the mangroves and tidal water was so different than the swamp she'd grown up in but this…this part was more familiar. Bringing buried memories to the surface. Grieving for her parents' deaths and of course losing Gator the way she had.

But hearing the cicadas singing, smelling the rotting vegetation and seeing the sun setting through the branches of the live oak was different. This was every summer evening she'd experienced as a kid and early teenager. All the stuff that she'd forgotten.

Meanwhile her needlessly expensive flip-flops were wearing into the top of her feet. She knew her mama would have said to take them off. Shoes like that weren't meant for the swamp.

But she didn't want to let another layer of the woman she'd become slip away.

"What about here?"

Torn back into the present, she glanced at the area he was pointing to. It was high enough that they'd be safe from ground animals and probably from being spotted by any of the cartel members.

"Yeah, that looks good. Want me to check it out and clear some of the area so we have enough room to pitch the tent?"

"Go for it. I'm going to scout around down here and make sure that we haven't left any obvious tracks."

She heard him move away. That was one thing she really liked about Xander: he respected her enough to trust her skills and not keep watch over her at all times.

Walking around, she found the right place. She cleared a pretty large area but tried to make it look organic. She tried to move a log that was sort of in the clearing she made, but it was too heavy for her. God, she was really out of shape.

Well, she was definitely going to start working out when she got home. But then she almost laughed at the ridiculousness of that statement. It was as if she anticipated she'd be on the run like this again.

But, what if she was?

What kind of survivor wasn't prepared for every situation?

Be easy, girl.

Her daddy's voice seemed to whisper to her on the humid breeze that blew through the trees. *Be easy.* Daddy said that all the time when one of them had gotten wound up. Just be easy. It was a simple order. It meant calm down and take a breath. But she'd been breathing herself into a coma in her real life in Miami, and being here, being the opposite of easy made her feel something again.

Alive, for sure.

It had been a long time since she'd snapped at someone or allowed herself to just be. Not to carefully filter every single feeling she had through some kind of strainer so that all that was left was someone who was bland and boring. A woman who tried to look like everyone else and blend in.

"Will it work?"

She glanced over at him. Xander stood at the base of the clearing, scratching a bite on his neck and waiting. "Yes."

"I couldn't move that log but maybe you can?" she asked.

Shrugging out of his pack, he put it in the center of the clearing and then moved toward the log. Her breath caught in her throat and her heart beat faster, watching him move. He was so physical. It was impossible not to look at him. His muscles bulged in his arms, and she knew his strength and wanted to feel them around her. She was staring at him but couldn't stop.

Their eyes met and that heat that had been between them under the pack-raft was back. The irritation and

"Is the swamp like the forest where the animals go quiet if another threat shows up?" he asked her as he pushed his pack into the tent. She bent and put her purse inside of the tent and then he motioned for her to climb in.

"Yes, animals go quiet when they sense a threat."

She made no move to enter the tent, just stood there for a long moment. Looking down into her face, he saw the effects of the day, slight reddish from too much sun and wind, the fatigue around her eyes, but she was still so damned beautiful everything masculine in him went on alert. Normally he made himself into someone less sexual when he was working, ignoring his baser demands and the attraction he sometimes felt toward his clients.

And maybe it was the bugs, heat and swamp or at least he wanted it to be, but he was struggling to do that with Obie.

He wanted to check his phone but after telling her she couldn't contact her district attorney friend, he wasn't sure how she'd take that. "I'm going to check in with my team. They should have some information for us. I know I asked you not to—"

"It's fine," she said. "For now it's fine. And you did say you might have something to read the SD card."

"Let's get into the tent."

She climbed in first. He forced his eyes away from her backside as she crawled in, but it was too late. He'd already seen the sweet curve of her ass and couldn't get that image out of his mind. He took an extra moment to check their surroundings before he followed her into the tent.

She had her purse next to her and she sat cross-legged on the floor with her arms around herself. Her shorts and tank top were suited to the day, but now that it was nightfall, a slight chill crept around them. "Want my shirt?"

"Why?"

"You seem cold. I've got a button-down in my bag that you could put on to keep yourself warm," he said.

"Thanks."

He dug it out and handed it to her, then turned on his phone to see if Lee or Van had gotten back to them.

He had a text from Van.

You really stepped in it. Situation is in flux. Stay low. Will see you at the marina when you get there. Not sure who to trust. Cartel dangerous.

He texted his boss back.

Assistant district attorney Crispin Tallman is working with Aaron to clear his name. Have the SD card. More cartel members were on our trail earlier this afternoon. Should be at the marina midday tomorrow.

Van answered immediately.

That's good news. Will reach out to the assistant district attorney. You good for the night?

Xander sent a thumbs-up back to his boss.

"Van's going to get in touch with Tallman. He said the situation is in flux."

"What's that mean?"

"That there are moving parts and he can't read them all," Xander said. He didn't like the sound of that any more than Obie's facial expression said she did. Aaron's information was the key to all of this. He pulled out his tech bag and looked around for the dongle he could attach to his phone and then insert the SD card in the other side.

"Let me see the SD card."

She opened her purse and pulled out the drybag he'd given her what felt like days ago instead of merely hours. She took the card out of the bag and handed it to him.

He shifted his bag around and then sat down.

"I'm nervous."

He glanced over at her.

She shrugged. She looked small with his big shirt draped around her body. Her arms were still around her waist; she was keeping it together and had been since that moment in the rain. That one moment he was trying his damnedest not to dwell on, but it was hard not to.

He wanted to pull her back against his body. Take her mouth under his again and kiss her until they both no longer remembered they were in the swamp and running for their lives.

He wanted to give them both something to think about that wasn't a drug cartel, family and death. But he also knew if he did that, if he compromised himself, he might screw things up and put her in danger. That wasn't something he was willing to do. He was the only one keeping her safe and he didn't take that duty lightly.

No matter how much he burned to pleasure her.

No matter how much his body demanded that he touch her.

He was having the hardest time not pushing that one silky-looking curl that kept falling forward against her cheek back behind her ear.

He literally balled his hand into a fist so he wouldn't touch her.

"The card," she said, holding it out to him.

Crap.

He opened his hand palm up, and her small finger rested against his palm, sending chills up his arm and heat spreading down his torso to his groin. The SD card dropped into the center of his hand but he was afraid to try to take it and put it in the card reader while he was touching her. He might drop it. He wanted to drop it and just turn his hand over and tug her off balance and against him.

But he didn't. He reached for the iron control he'd been lauded for and pulled it around him. Wrapping himself away from this woman.

Chapter 12

The closeness of the shelter made her feel safe. His critter-proof tent was surprisingly comfy. He had pulled out a packing cube of his clothes that he offered for her to use as a pillow. She set it to one side waiting while he held the SD card in one hand.

She was afraid to see what was on it. Afraid of what it would mean once she had that knowledge. He took the card, putting it into the reader while setting his phone aside. Their eyes met and then he just shook his head.

"Why did you have to agree to help Aaron?"

"I told you. Family," she said.

He cursed under his breath and then took her hand in his, lifting it to his mouth and kissing her palm. A shiver of awareness went through her, making her breasts feel full and her nipples tighten. This was what she needed, maybe more than whatever information was on that card. The information that the cartel was willing to kill for. She shifted up on her knees and leaned forward, willing away the fear that had been chasing her all day.

Xander had been reluctant to kiss each of the times

they had. She felt like she'd been the one driving that. But this time, he tugged on her wrist and pulled her off balance until she fell into his arms. Those powerful arms that she'd been admiring as she watched him building the shelter for them, making sure they were safe.

He held her, his body smelling of the swamp and summer and sweat. It was a heady combination that turned her on like nothing else had. No one else had in a long time. She put her hands on his shoulders and tipped her head back until she could see his eyes. He watched her mouth. She saw a wildness in him for the first time.

It was exciting to see her calm, cool, self-appointed bodyguard enthralled by her. She started to say something. To tell him that she wanted this too. But his mouth came down on hers. Hard and demanding. She opened her mouth under his, his tongue sweeping over hers and thrusting deep into her mouth.

She held on to his shoulders, and he kept her close with one hand on her back and the other one slipped under the button-down shirt he'd given her earlier. His touch moved to the hem of her tank top where it had ridden up from the waistband of her shorts. She felt his fingers moving over her skin, rubbing against the exposed flesh, as the intensity of the kiss changed.

He took his time, his tongue moving more leisurely against her, his finger following the same movement. Her skin felt so sensitized by his touch that chill bumps spread up her chest to her neck. His hand on her back shifted around, balling the fabric of the shift he'd given her until she felt his hand on her back. He pushed her tank top up and then the heat of his palm was on her bare skin.

She shivered and for a moment just let herself enjoy being touched by this man. His hands and his mouth held her. She opened her eyes, moving her fingers against the side of his throat and up to his jawline. He lifted his head and their eyes met.

She felt like he wanted to say something, but maybe he wasn't sure what to say. She got to her knees and straddled him. Letting her thighs slide along the outside of his legs and keeping her hands where they were framing his face. She lowered her body until the center of her rubbed against his erection.

Maybe he was going to say they should stop out of caution, but she didn't want to. The reasons why she wanted him didn't need repeating to herself. She knew what she needed. She needed to feel alive and to forget for a little while why they were together in this intimate little cocoon he'd created for them.

He started to speak but she brought her mouth down on his, caught his lower lip between her teeth and bit gently, sucking his lower lip into her mouth as she rocked her hips over his erection.

He groaned and the hand on her back moved lower to her butt, grasping at it and driving her harder against him as his hips moved up into her body.

She tossed her head back as he thrust against her and he felt his mouth on her neck, sucking against her skin and driving her mad. She rocked harder against him and he continued to drive up against her. His hand on her butt tightened and he brought his other hand to her waist, driving her harder and harder against him as he continued to thrust up against her.

Her orgasm washed over her, making her shudder and shake his arms as he brought her mouth down on his so she could taste more of him as she climaxed.

He cursed and pulled back from her, but she kept moving against him, until he buried his face in her neck, encouraging her to continue rocking against him. Sated for the moment, she collapsed against him for a minute. She lay there in his arms for a few more moments before he lifted his head.

"Well, that was unexpected."

She gave a soft laugh. "Understatement of the year. I'm not going to say I'm sorry. I wanted you and I would have liked you inside of me."

But she knew he wouldn't have done that.

"Obie."

That was all he said, just her name. He lifted her off his lap and turned away, busying himself with something in his pack.

What was it about her that made him regret every physical touch?

Xander was rock-hard. Hearing Obie say she wanted him inside of her made him even stiffer. But he'd already decided that wasn't happening. He was trying to keep every bit of his control, but each moment in her presence made it so much tougher.

She just wasn't someone he could resist. He had met a lot of women he admired and he hadn't been like this.

She was different. Which was why he was trying not to give in to his base temptations.

He knew she watched him. And there were only so many things he could shuffle around in his pack. He was stalling. His hand touched a deck of cards and he pulled them out as he turned to face her.

"What is going on with you?"

"I'm trying to be sensible."

"I thought we had gone past sensible. We've shared so much today…"

They had; he didn't need her to remind him all they'd been through together. But he felt like today might end up being the easiest day they had. Van's text was worrying. Was Aaron in deeper than he'd let on, or was someone Aaron trusted betraying him?

At least it wasn't Obie. It seemed far-fetched that she'd be involved with the cartel she thought had killed her parents.

Or had she just said that to throw him off? He thought about the SD card, which they hadn't read yet because he'd been distracted by their make-out session.

Was she trying to keep him from seeing something on it?

The moment that thought entered his mind he knew it was ridiculous. Who sets themselves up to get shot at? Especially a civilian who clearly had no training. He put the pack of cards on the floor of the tent. He pulled his phone back to him. "Let's find out what's on here."

He opened the reader on his phone and noticed there were several files on the card. Obie came closer, but not too close, which immediately confirmed he'd hurt her by making out with her and then putting up walls. He was going to have to talk to her about it, but right now the card had information that they both needed to see.

There were two photo albums with file names that were all numbers—dates were his best guess. The dates were from the last two weeks. He opened the first one and it looked like a strip mall of some sort.

"That's the coffee shop," Obie said.

She leaned over him, careful not to touch him when she was normally such a tactile person. He turned and started to say something, but she shook her head.

"Later. See if there are more photos of the coffee shop. Do you think this means he was dealing out of the shop?"

He had no idea. And wouldn't until they had a fuller picture of what was on the card. He opened more photos and saw that there was one of Obie laughing while she talked to a customer. She looked very different than she did right now. It was a photo of a beautiful woman with straight black hair, red lipstick, still gorgeous as she was now…but different.

"Why are all these photos of the shop on there?" she asked, more to herself.

They kept moving through the photos and eventually a car pulled up and the next photo was of Aaron.

Xander's breath caught. He hadn't seen his brother in ten years. He'd filled out from the twenty-four-year-old young adult he'd been. His hair was long, not too dissimilar to Xander's own style, and he was beefy but still a few inches shorter than Xander. In the photo, Aaron was in the process of taking off his sunglasses and seemed to be looking toward the photographer.

"I'm confused," Obie said. "Is he trying to get this back because it shows the coffee shop? I haven't seen anything that Aaron can use to cut a deal."

"Me either. But we haven't seen everything," Xander said. "I wonder if Aaron swiped this because it had photos of you and the shop on there."

"To protect us?" That note of worry was back in her voice and he knew that it wasn't just her picture being on the SD card that made her nervous.

He had done his own share of making scared.

"Maybe," he said, then turned to her. "I'm sorry."

She shook her head. "Don't be nice to me right now. Just be the bodyguard," she said.

She needed more from him than just being a bodyguard. They had gotten closer, and once he'd completely given in to temptation and taken her in his arms, she'd seen that as a bond between them. This woman shared her knowledge and skills of the swamp as well as her fears that someone had murdered her parents. She expected more from the people she shared her past with.

She deserved more too. He owed her the truth and he would give it to her, find a way to assuage her fears and make her trust him again. The files and the cartel's response meant that Obie might know more than she realized, and the danger to her might have been there all along, not just when she'd walked into Aaron's house on Key Largo to retrieve this card.

"You deserve—"

"To see more photos," she said. "Just show me what else is on there. I'm going to need to let Hilda know. I don't want anyone else to be in danger."

"Me either," he said, respecting her wishes and moving through the rest of the photos in the first album, which showed Aaron talking to another man in the alley behind the coffee shop. The man's back was to them and he had a tattoo on the back of his neck that was hard to make out.

She thought nothing would take her mind off what had just happened between them, but seeing the pictures of the coffee shop as well as Bea, Hilda and herself worried her. Aaron in particular looked different in the photos that had captured him. That carefree dishwasher she normally saw looked pensive and tense as he'd gotten out of his car.

"Do you think he knew he was being watched?"

"Probably or at least was taking some precautions. Do you recognize this guy?" He pointed to the last photo in the file, which showed the back of another man. The man wore a dark gray suit and had a tattoo that showed just above the collar on the left-hand side.

"No one dressed like that came into the coffee shop while I was working. And I can't really see the tattoo. Can you zoom in on it?"

He tried but the lines weren't any clearer; the collar on the man's suit jacket hid most of it.

Xander zoomed back out and opened the data file next, which was encrypted. He closed it and went to the next file, which had more photos from the file extensions, but these were encrypted too.

"So all we can see are pictures of the coffee shop and Aaron. Aaron must know the key to unlock the files," Obie said.

"That would be my guess. I'm going to send the files to my team. I'll ask Van to send someone to your coffee shop to watch the people who work there."

Van, his boss. The one he thought was going to be able to help them once they got to the marina. She was putting a lot of trust in this man who kept putting up barriers despite the fire that raged between them, and she was tired, hungry and hurt. Not a good combo.

For a minute, just the barest of one, she thought of Aunt Karen, who would tell her to keep her opinions to herself and go to sleep. But then she shoved them away. Aunt Karen wasn't here. She was in the freaking swamp. Obie wasn't the civilized, ordinary woman in those surveillance photos right now. She was the wild swamp girl again.

"Great. I'm glad your boss will watch out for them," she said.

"Yeah."

He put the reader and his phone back in the drybag and handed her the SD card, which she took and turned to put it away as well.

When she turned back around he had a deck of cards in his hands and was opening it. "I think I mentioned that I suck at personal relationships."

"Yeah, but I hadn't realized how that would impact me," she said. "I am really close to losing my temper."

"I can see that. You're like that lightning that flashed across the sky earlier. I can feel you singeing the hair on my arms."

"That's not all I'm going to singe."

"I had a feeling. How about we high-card and I'll answer any question you have for me no matter how personal?"

"And what will I do?" She liked the idea of him having to answer her.

"The same. I have a feeling there are things you still haven't told me."

"Fine. Let's go."

He shuffled the cards and then offered the deck to her. "Ladies first."

Obie took a small stack and held it next to her legs. Xander pulled another small stack and lifted his toward her.

"King of spades."

She lifted her card: three of clubs.

"So you lose. Why did you stop when we were making out? Do you just not want to be with me? Were you doing it to be nice?" All of the questions sort of fell out of her mouth and she knew she should have asked him about Aaron and the photos or something else. Anything else.

"Ah well, because I shouldn't have let it get started. I want to be with you, Obie, but we're in danger, and a man making love to a woman while being chased by a deadly drug cartel is a shitty bodyguard. You distract me and tempt me more than you realize. Keeping you safe and alive is my number-one priority. I'm sorry I let things get out of hand."

"That sounds… I'm not sure if I can trust you."

"You can," he said and it sounded like a promise.

She wasn't sure if she wanted to.

"Next," he said. He won the next round of High Card.

"The man with his back to the camera reminds you of someone. Who?"

She thought he hadn't noticed but shouldn't have been surprised that he had. The man looked like her father. A man she knew was dead. But his height and his shoulders weren't the same, nor were his military buzz cut and that small mark that she thought was a tattoo. It was how he carried himself, a sense of alertness and confidence that harkened back to her dad. When they'd zoomed in she'd realized it might be a birthmark.

"It's nothing."

"We said honesty."

"Yeah, we did. He looks like my dad from the back, but he's definitely dead because Gator and I had to identify the bodies when they were brought in," she said. "So I know that's not him."

"Does he have any brothers?"

"No. And I don't honestly think that's my dad. He just holds himself the same way. Like a cop," she said. "I think if I had to guess…that man is a cop."

Chapter 13

Xander wasn't sure what it meant that Aaron had been talking to someone that looked like a cop. Rick, who worked on his team, was a former DEA agent. Given the cartel's involvement, maybe he should ask Rick to reach out and see if he could find anything.

"I think you're right about it being a cop," Xander said.

"Does that mean Aaron is working with the cops or is that how they got the information to arrest him? I mean that guy isn't pretending to be a buyer," she said. "He sticks out in our neighborhood and like I said I never saw him."

"One of our team used to work with the DEA. I'm going to reach out to him and ask him to do some digging," Xander said.

He pulled his phone out and texted Rick, who answered back immediately.

On it. Also heads-up the entire team is heading your way. I will check in at the local DEA office when we land.

The entire team.

He just thumbs-upped Rick's message and then opened his chat with Van.

Why is the entire team coming here?

Shit is getting real. That encrypted file is hard to break and we are working on it. But the photos of the girl and your brother. The meta data shows they weren't taken by your brother. So someone was watching him and the shop. You stay focused on keeping the girl safe. The team is going to find out what the heck is going on.

Xander tossed his phone down. He didn't want the team involved in this. But he knew there was no stopping Van once he made up his mind.

I'll pay for the team to investigate.

Not happening.

Why not?

It's family.

Family.

Not yours.

You are. Not arguing. See you tomorrow.

"Everything okay?" Obie asked.

"Yeah. Rick's going to check in with the local DEA

office and see what he can find. My entire team is en route to us."

"Why?"

"Those encrypted files. I guess they are hard to crack or something worrying is on them," he said.

He had nothing more to add to it. He was relieved that Rick was checking the DEA angle.

"Could Aaron be working for them?" she asked.

"Maybe. The DEA could have been in touch to try to turn him—maybe that's what happened."

"And someone found out, that's why they staked out the shop?" she asked.

He glanced over at her; she still held herself stiff with him but she was relaxing more and more as they talked about what was going on with the card and the cartel chasing them.

"Maybe."

"In TV shows that's always the case," she said. "That would be nice. Then I wouldn't have been wrong about Aaron being a nice guy."

Nice wasn't something that Xander ever gave any thought to but he got what she was saying. "Aaron can be a nice guy to you and still be a criminal. Doesn't mean you read him wrong."

She shrugged, chewing her lower lip between her teeth, reminding him of the way those teeth had felt on his own lip when she'd sucked it into his mouth. He turned his head away and looked down at his phone for a distraction.

"Seems that as the daughter of a sheriff I should be able to recognize the bad guys," she said.

She sounded a little bit surly and he hid a smile. "Yeah, but it doesn't work that way."

"How does it work?" she asked. "Plus how do you know?"

"I read a book on it."

He had read many books on psychology and interpersonal relationships, as well as family dynamics and how they affected people as they became adults and entered the workplace. He couldn't be a bodyguard if he didn't know how to analyze the people close to his charges. Everyone had something complicated simmering under the surface.

"What did it say?"

"Just that we sometimes see what we want to see. That's how magicians and illusionists are successful. When Aaron came to you for work, he presented himself like a down-on-his-luck guy who needed a gig. That's what you saw. There's no fault in you."

She crossed her arms over her chest again and shook her head. "I don't like it. I've always thought I was a good judge of character."

She probably was. In her daily life he'd guess not many people were trying to deceive her. "That's why Aaron was able to fool you, you're used to relying on your instincts and they have always been right or right most of the time. So when someone who is used to deceiving shows up you see only what they are showing you."

"I don't like it. Makes me feel gullible."

She was naive in a way because she believed so strongly that doing the right thing would get her the results she wanted. And in her daily life that was all she needed to do. But in this world, the one where cartels and drug dealers and the DEA crossed, it was going to take a lot more than doing the right thing.

He didn't tell her that because he knew that wouldn't make her feel better. And he had her back. He had one objective since he'd scooped her up and ran for the boat. That was to keep her safe and alive.

But she was still worried.

"How long did you say Aaron work for you?"

"Three weeks," she said. "Why?"

"I bet if he'd worked for you longer you would have seen signs of things that didn't add up. As you said earlier he was more of an acquaintance than a good friend," Xander pointed out. "I wouldn't rule out your gut just yet."

She shifted around, curling her legs underneath her. He had a small camp blanket, which he dug out of his pack and tossed over her. "Try to get some rest."

"Are you going to?"

"Not yet," he said. He didn't really need a lot of sleep. Probably a sign of his profession, but he had to be on alert when he was on a job. A threat to his clients didn't stick to a schedule and a certain bedtime. The cartel would be the same. He wasn't going to rest until he got to the bottom of this and Obie was safe.

He'd said to sleep and she was pretending to, but she wasn't sure she actually could. Everything about the day was rushing through her head. She regretted that she'd given in to that need for closeness and kissed Xander.

It made her feel the way she had the first time she'd had sex. She'd been seventeen. Gator had been gone for a few months and Aunt Karen had been demanding things Obie wasn't sure she wanted to give. Obie had felt alone and scared and had thought that she'd find the connection she'd been missing in her boyfriend's arms.

But she hadn't. The sex had been okay. Fair enough, they'd both been new to it and hadn't really known what they were meant to do. But when it was over, even though Bo had held her, she hadn't felt that closeness.

If only she'd remembered that before she'd allowed herself to give in to her instincts and kiss Xander. You'd think that at thirty she'd have more sense than she did at seventeen.

Sex had just created another ripple in her self-confidence. That same confidence that had taken a hit when Aaron had called her from jail. The Quentin men were really pushing her to examine the way she looked at men around her.

She couldn't blame Xander for the way he'd reacted. Either during their making out or after. Well after… She shook her head and rolled onto her back. He'd turned the light out and was sitting quietly near the zippered opening of the tent. She could see the stiffness of his back.

She wished he'd magically turn into someone who would take her away from this nightmare she found herself in. Not realistic at all, she knew that. Didn't mean she wasn't still hoping to wake up at home in her own bed.

"Why did you kiss me?"

Startled, she hadn't realized he knew she was awake.

A part of her wanted to say something that would hurt him. But that was petty and below her. He hadn't asked for any of this either.

"I like you," she said. "You make me feel safe and I don't know, I just did. Why did you kiss me back?"

He turned around, still cross-legged on the floor but now facing her. "I want you."

"I wasn't exactly saying no."

"Yeah. I know. That made it even harder to stop. But I'm not so out of control yet that I don't know what's right."

"And sex with me wouldn't be?"

"I didn't say that."

"I know. I just… I'm feeling odd. I should have pretended to be asleep when you spoke to me."

He moved over to where she was and sat down next to her. "I'm glad you didn't. And *odd* sounds about right for the day you've had."

She nodded, not sure why he'd come closer. He smelled of bug spray now, along with the heady mix of their surroundings. But it wasn't an unpleasant odor. Part of her liked it.

"I don't want to add to the burden of this day," he said.

She understood what he was saying. Her trying to have sex with him had been a reaction to so many things. She liked the way he was so contained and then he'd shared little tidbits of himself with her.

But in reality would they see each other after they got out of the swamp?

Probably not.

His life was miles away and he had no time for relationships. She wasn't entirely sure she would want to be with him after they got out of here anyway. Wasn't sure if she could trust her own judgment. "I'm sorry. Let's put the kiss down to just being happy we were alive and not having to walk any more today."

"That would be sensible," he said.

She hated that word. Every decision that Aunt Karen had urged her to make since she'd come to live with her had been *sensible*. Or *logical*. The *right thing to do*. And the right thing hadn't healed her or solved her problems the way she'd hoped.

"Sensible sucks."

"It does. Seems like a compromise between two shitty choices."

"Exactly. When does anyone say *Do this thing that makes you happy*?" she asked.

"That's not what life is about," he said. "Or at least that's my impression."

"Yeah. I know. I guess almost dying today is making me reframe my life. That might seem melodramatic but maybe that's where I am."

He lay down next to her, stretching out and putting his hands behind his head. "I don't think it's OTT. Days like today force us to grow and change in a way that nothing else will."

"But you must be used to it," she said.

"To being shot at?"

"Mmm-hmm."

"As much as anyone can be used to that. But I meant unexpected accidents that force you off the path you thought you were on."

"Sounds like we aren't talking about me anymore," she said.

She wondered what had happened to him to make him a bodyguard. He'd told her about his brush with the law and about the SAS, but how did the kind man in the picture he'd shown her turn into this hardened warrior?

How did any of us become who we are?

He should have left well enough alone. Let Obie sleep, or pretend to, but he hadn't been able to stop thinking of her. He screwed up when he'd kissed her the way he had, knowing he couldn't let it go any further. The fact that they were being pursued by the cartel should have been enough of a boner-killer to keep him from touching her.

Even now, when he should be sitting by the tent opening on alert. Instead he was stretched out next to her. Talking. But he knew he wanted more. Wanted her under him. So that he could pretend for a few hours in the middle of this strange night that he didn't have regrets.

Regrets about Obie of course and how he'd kissed her and then pushed her away but also regrets about Aaron. The cop in the picture had thrown him. He

fear and memories disappeared, and all she could do was stare at his mouth. Wish that he'd kiss her again.

And more.

Everything in her was starting to awaken, the needs and desires she'd been denying suddenly demanding attention. And the fact that she had no idea what was going to happen to them tonight or tomorrow just fed the urgency in her. She reached out to touch his upper arm.

He flexed his muscle as he put his hand on her waist.

"Are you okay? I'll get the tent set up and then you can climb in and get some rest."

After a lifetime of what felt like rest that was the last thing she wanted. She wanted the excitement and even the danger that she felt around Xander because at last she felt alive.

Xander wasn't entirely sure that the was going to be make it through the entire night in the tent with Obie without taking her in his arms again. His control was legendary when he was on the job. Kenji always teased him that he was an iron man when it came to keeping his emotions safely locked up. It was a good thing his friend wasn't here now.

Whenever he touched her, his mind went blank and his body took over.

He dropped his hand as she nodded.

He made quick work of setting up the tent in the area she'd found, which offered them a lot of cover. Once he had it set up, he put some of the branches back around it to help it blend in better. It was getting dark now and the noise of the swamp was louder.

knew better than to make snap judgments but somehow it had seemed easier to assume Aaron had become a midlevel drug dealer than to look beyond his old anger and pettiness toward his brother and be logical.

Sensible like Obie had said was some kind of double-edged sword that left him feeling unsatisfied.

"So?"

He'd said too much, which was why he usually kept his mouth shut. Perhaps his subconscious wanted to tell her about his brothers and what happened to Tony. Not just Aaron, but the other two as well. His part in the incident that had changed all of their lives.

Helping Aaron was never going to be just a favor from him. Coming here was always going to involve more than he wanted to give. Maybe if he had contacted Aaron sooner, his brother wouldn't have gotten into this mess.

"You must really be keeping something deep down. I get it. That's how I felt for the last decade or so about the swamp. But today when we were in that boat and there was nowhere else to go… I just had no choice but to face the past and the memories I'd buried there."

"You think I'm hiding?"

"I know you are," she said. "That picture you showed me to confirm you were Aaron's brother is old, and the four boys in that picture looked like they'd do anything for each other. Something happened to change that, Xander. You don't have to tell me what it is, but I think that's what you're hiding from."

She wasn't wrong. He didn't want to talk about it.

But the past was suddenly there in the forefront of his mind as it hadn't been when he was working. "Maybe I work so much so I don't slow down and have to face the past."

"That's what I do. I take extra shifts, volunteer at the homeless kitchen two blocks from the shop and just keep myself running until I collapse. I was where you are yesterday."

"Today really didn't leave you many choices, did it?"

"It didn't," she said, rolling to her side, and he turned his head in his hands to look at her. There wasn't really any light or even ambient light in the tent.

His vision was pretty good and his eyes had adjusted to the darkness so he could make out her shape. He had memorized her face earlier so he knew what she looked like even now. But what she felt, how to respond... Not even full-on light would help with that.

Today though he'd felt like he was starting to know Obie. Not that it made it easier for him to open up and talk to her.

"Do you wish you'd said no when Aaron asked you to retrieve the card?" he asked.

"Yes and no. I mean I couldn't have said no once he mentioned the cartel. I wish... I sort of wish I hadn't hired him. If he'd gone to work someplace else then I wouldn't be here."

"So once you hired him this path was inevitable."

"Yeah. I don't know if I said but Aaron reminds me of my brother, Gator. And I have lost him. I thought...

maybe I could save Gator by helping Aaron. Not in real life but in…"

She trailed off and he got it. She was trying to get rid of regret. Trying not to be haunted by it like him.

"Is it working? Do you feel less regret about Gator?" he asked. Somehow it was easier to have this conversation in the dark. He wouldn't have pushed her this way while they'd been walking. In part because of being followed and the threat from the swamp. But here in the dark it felt almost okay to ask.

"I wish I could say yes. But I don't think so. Aaron isn't Gator and he's also not the man I thought he was. I guess that's a pretty solid no."

He rolled toward her. "You didn't do this for Aaron— you did it for yourself. You made a different choice than you did with Gator…or at least that's what I'm guessing. Doesn't mean the outcome is different for either Gator or Aaron but is it something you can live with? Isn't that something to be proud of?"

She reached out and touched his hand. Just her cold fingers against the back of his. "I hadn't thought of it that way. But now that you've mentioned it I do feel better. Last time… I let my aunt influence me and my decision. This time… Well, from the moment I saw Aaron I had to hire him. Mainly because I don't know what happened to Gator and maybe if I hired this broken, lost man someone who ran across Gator might help him."

She rolled onto her back again. "God, I know how that sounds. Sort of woo-woo and like there is some big karmic ledger book that someone is keeping track of and my deeds will help my brother. Nuts, right?"

"Nah. Sounds exactly right for someone who has a complicated relationship with their sibling," he said.

Chapter 14

Obie drifted off to sleep and Xander watched over her through the night. When the first hints of dawn started to light the interior of the tent he shook her awake, taking her in as she stretched before sitting upright.

"I'm surprised I slept."

He wasn't. She had been exhausted and wrung out from the day. "Hopefully tonight you'll be in your own bed."

"Hopefully."

They got out of the tent and Obie went first to have some privacy in the bushes. Xander was on alert as he collapsed the tent and rolled it back up. Obie had folded his shirt up neatly and had taken the spare undershirt he'd packed to change out of her tank top from the day before.

She returned the clearing with his shirt knotted to the left side of her waist. "Thanks for the shirt. I wish I'd worn better shoes. Next time…"

She trailed off and sort of laughed. "I hope there won't be anything like this again, but in the back of my mind I have a list of things I'm going to start carry-

ing in my purse. And I definitely won't leave the house
wearing just flip-flops again."

"That's why I'm lugging this thing around."

She glanced over at his pack. "I like the idea of all
that stuff, but it's a bit much for me to carry every day.
I'd settle for some toothpaste and maybe coffee."

"I have some instant and we could use the camp
stove if you want to make some," he said. "You're sort
of the expert."

"Okay. Do we have water?"

"My filtration bottle is full. We can fill it up when
we get down to the lake and let the filter do its thing.
If you don't want to have coffee that's okay too." He
wanted to get them moving and away from the camp
now that it was daylight. But he knew that sometimes
in a situation like this, the little things helped to make
it easier for someone like Obie.

"I'm good for now. When we get to the marina
hopefully they'll have some."

"It might not be until later this afternoon," he warned
her.

"That's fine. Go and get changed. I'm slightly jeal-
ous that you have an entire change of clothes," she said
teasingly.

"The gun is on the top of pack. Same as last time,
there's a round in the chamber and the safety is on.
Just click off the safety, point and shoot."

Her face got tight with tension but she nodded.
He left her a moment later. He moved quickly. There
wasn't really a place to wash up despite being the
swamp. The parts they'd been in hadn't been the clean,

clear springs that ran through different sections of the Everglades. He used the wipes he'd had in his pack to refresh himself and put on some deodorant before donning his fresh clothes and starting back toward the camp.

He stopped when he heard voices. He reached for his knife, which he kept in a sheath in the pocket of his utility shorts. He pulled it out, moving quickly back to Obie so she wasn't alone when the hikers got to her.

The voices made it seem as if the people weren't too far away. He entered the camp and Obie had the gun held loosely by her side and was turned to face the sound of the talking he'd heard. He came up beside her.

"Thank God you're back. Here," she said, handing him the gun.

He took it from her. "Want the knife?"

"No. I'd probably just hurt myself with it."

"Fair enough. Get ready to go. I'm not sure if they are with the cartel or not but if we move we can put some distance between us."

She nodded. "They are back toward West Lake."

"I know—we'll have to go around. Can you navigate us into the swamp and away from them and then we can double back?"

"I'll try," she said. "Good thing we decided to skip coffee."

"Yup. Let's go."

She put her purse across her body again and he shrugged into his backpack. Obie led the way deeper into the underbrush they'd used the night before to hide their tent. She kept walking until they were obscured by the dense roots of cypress trees. He put his hand on her shoulder to stop her.

The voices were getting closer and he wanted a look at whoever it was. Obie seemed to be on the same page. She turned toward them as well. She had the drybag with her phone in her hand.

"Should I try to get a picture of them?" she whispered to him.

"If you can," he said.

She took her phone from the drybag, quietly stowing the bag. He noticed her screen saver was a painting of an orange blossom. She used her face to unlock the phone and then tapped the camera app. She zoomed in so that their campsite was in focus. They both waited, and a few minutes later a man and a woman entered the trail, looked around and then stepped into their campsite from the night before.

They sat on the log he'd moved and took out a thermos of coffee and both drank from it. Obie had snapped a few photos of them.

He still had no idea if they were just hikers or if they were with the cartel or another party. Though Xander was tempted to rule out a third party. Thus far they hadn't seen anything to make him think there were players looking for the SD card.

The couple finished their coffee and then stood and looked carefully around at the ground. Xander knew he'd wiped all trace of the presence from the area before he'd gone to change. They wouldn't find anything left behind, and Obie was at home in the swamp and had so far been really great at not leaving a trail.

The couple moved on a few minutes later.

For now, they were safe.

They were silent as they continued walking. Obie led the way with Xander occasionally tapping her arm to tell her to change directions. She wanted to be alert for anything in the swamp that she'd recognize as a danger that Xander might miss but she couldn't help her fear of other people.

Something new to add to the list of things that she was going to need to talk to a therapist about. Aunt Karen had taken her and Gator to see one after their parents had died, but Obie hadn't been ready to talk and had started skipping the sessions. She was pretty sure Gator had done the same thing. Eventually Aunt Karen had confronted them about it and told them she wasn't going to keep wasting money if they weren't interested in being helped.

So she'd stopped going. But now she almost wished she hadn't. The last twenty-four hours had shown her how much she had never dealt with. Grief was one helluva thing and it never really went away. It was just softer now. Being in the swamp, thinking of Mama and Daddy didn't hurt the way it used to. But she still missed them.

She didn't need a therapist to tell her that. But she could have used one after Gator left. Obie knew she'd never really be able to forgive herself for letting him go alone. She knew their parents would have wanted them to stick together.

But the unknown had been scarier than staying at

Aunt Karen's with the rules. The woman she was now, who was walking through the swamp with a big man with a gun and a knife at her side, wanted to snort at teenage Obie.

Fear manifested itself in all kinds of ways.

She put her hand up to stop them. The water had been rising and was at her knees now. The area in front of them looked as if it might be getting deeper. The lake was to the southwest of them and she wanted to get to the lake and the marina.

She wanted to be someplace safe and away from everyone who wanted the SD card or her dead.

"Do you think we can start doubling back? It's deeper that way and unless we have an airboat I don't feel safe continuing into that area."

Xander looked at the back trail and then at his compass. He took a few minutes to check the map and the trail again before he put his phone away.

"That should be fine. We are making pretty good progress and we've only gone about forty minutes out of our way if my calculations are correct."

Which she'd lay money on them being right. Xander didn't make many missteps, not when it came to this.

"Okay. With the tide rising I'm not sure what we'll encounter so just watch your feet as we go shallower."

He looked like he was going to say something and then changed his mind. She almost pushed him to say what was on his mind but then stopped. The kiss had been her misstep. Her trying to hold on to someone when life got overwhelming. This morning she'd made up her mind to rely on herself. Just like Destiny's Child had said: *I depend on me.*

She walked south and felt more confident with each step. She started to pick up the pace, the water sluicing around her flip-flops with each step but the sand underfoot was no longer sinking. That was a very a good sign they were getting to firmer land. The swamp was complex and diverse and despite the knowledge she had from her upbringing and the books she'd read there was still so much she didn't know.

She carefully wove them through both mangroves until she saw what looked like a dry path.

It would be nice to stand on firm ground. She took a step toward the path but Xander grabbed the waistband of her shorts and pulled her down into the water using the mangrove roots as cover as a group of four people emerged on the path.

They looked like a mix between the duo from the old camp earlier and the cartel men from the day before. There was no talking or joking between them. They had on khaki shirts and camo utility pants. One guy had his head shaved and had on aviator sunglasses.

They moved in a pattern, searching the area. There was something in the man closest to her that reminded her of her father. Maybe another cop? She looked at Xander but he shook his head. He wasn't trusting anyone other than his team, she guessed.

The water was up to her shoulders so there was no way to get her camera out; she just stared at the foursome trying to remember details. And as they moved past the spot that she and Xander were hiding in, she noticed that the woman closest to them wore a side-arm holstered at her waist.

They had to be police or with law enforcement.

Why wasn't Xander approaching them?

Maybe this group was looking for them and here to help.

Once again she tipped her head toward them and he gave her a hard glare and a short negative shake of his head.

As soon as they were alone she was going to confront him about this. If they were cops they would protect the two of them. Was Xander afraid to admit he needed help keeping her safe?

Xander knew that Obie didn't agree with him that they should stay hidden. She wasn't exactly subtle, and after the third time that she pinched him he knew she was probably going to let him have it when they were finally able to talk. The people looked like law enforcement, which was probably why Obie was keen to talk to them.

But the photos on Aaron's SD card were only a part of the puzzle. And right now Xander was still struggling to figure out if those pictures were important pieces or a distraction. The only person he 100 percent trusted in the swamp was right next to him. She'd come in with him. She'd saved him from being attacked by snakes and crocs, so as far as he was concerned trusting her was a no-brainer.

But these other people? No way.

He wasn't sure if Aaron had been working with the

guy in the suit or if he had been arrested by the guy in the suit, an undercover cop. He should have asked Obie if she remembered what day it was that those photos were taken.

The group moved on after the leader, the bald man in the front, heard from someone via his earpiece.

Damn. These weren't just regular law enforcement and with equipment like that they had the look of some kind of elite team.

He wasn't sure that the team would be working with the cartel but he didn't rule it out either. As soon as they were clear and he felt it was safe, he motioned for her to move.

"Why didn't you let them know we were here? They looked like cops to me," she said, keeping her voice low and still moving cautiously as she led the way out of their cover.

"They look like an elite team. The kind that is hired by someone with a lot of money. I'd say ex–law enforcement. We don't know who sent them. It could be the cartel. They have money," Xander said.

"Or maybe your boss sent them," she said.

Definitely not. As much as they worked with law enforcement a lot in their gigs, Van didn't like working with mercenaries. And other private firms were technically his competitors. "He didn't."

"I'm tired, Xander. If those men can get us back to civilization I wouldn't mind taking a chance. I mean you have your gun… Sorry, I just realized I was thinking if they weren't on our side you could handle them. You're probably tired too."

"I am. If I thought there was a chance they were clean I might have taken the risk. But the truth is I don't know enough to risk it. Do you remember the photos of your shop and Aaron?"

She licked her dry lips and nodded before digging in her bag for her lip balm. "What about them?"

"Do you recall if they were taken on the day he was arrested?"

She considered his question as she found her lip balm and put it on. "I don't think so. Actually it looked like one of the first few days that Aaron started working for us. Why?"

"Just trying to rule out the possibility of him working with an agency or of them trying to turn him," Xander said. "But I don't think that can be done."

"Sorry I'm not more help. And for pinching you. You told me that your job is to keep me safe and you're doing that. I should have trusted you."

He almost smiled. She might have been ticked while they'd been hiding, but now that she was out of the water and on dry ground, she was being fair. He wished for the thousandth time she hadn't been dragged into this mess. But she was making the best of it.

"You should have. But it's okay. Even I wasn't sure if we should make contact," he said. "I'm never going to take any action that puts you in direct danger."

"Thanks for that. Would you have confronted them if you'd been alone?" she asked as they started walking again toward West Lake.

"Yes."

There was no question in his mind that he would

have used whatever means necessary to get information and get out of the swamp. "But I probably would have panicked the first time I saw that croc and gotten bit. So might not have been as tough on my own as you're thinking."

She shook her head as she adjusted the shoulder strap of her cross-body bag. "You would be. I don't think you would have disturbed the croc. You're too calm for that."

He wished he could really lay claim to the calmness she thought she saw in him. Doing a different job in any other part of the world might have allowed him the chance. But he was winging it with Obie, and it was training and skills and her knowledge of the swamp that was keeping them one step ahead of the cartel and this new player who was after them.

It was partially just dumb luck. But then again, Van always said Xander made his own luck.

He would keep Obie safe and deliver her to Van, and then he was going to start talking to the different parties and get the information he needed to solve this puzzle.

Chapter 15

Obie was hot as they continued walking through the swamp. Neither of them talked, but if Xander's mind was anything like hers then the silence wasn't restful. She couldn't help thinking about a third party being involved. What was Aaron into? It had been hard enough to swallow the drug cartel connection, but this seemed to be growing larger.

She couldn't help remembering that her father had been doing a hush-hush investigation when he'd been killed. Officer Wade had told them that he didn't trust the higher-ups.

All of which hadn't really meant much to her at the time. She'd been bereft with grief and not really concerned about her dad's workplace drama. But now she had to wonder if uncovering these memories was helping her make connections between law enforcement and the cartel. What part did Aaron play in it all?

She wanted to ask Xander his opinion, but she hesitated, knowing in her heart that she wanted to find something that would connect the cartel to her parents' deaths. Xander would be honest with her if she was pushing for something that wasn't there.

When they got to the east side of West Lake, she filled his water filtrating bottle while he got out the pack-raft.

"Do you think that the cartel could have ties to law enforcement?" she said, trying for casual and totally failing.

"Uh, maybe. Where's this coming from?"

She shrugged as she put the top back on the water bottle. "Was just thinking about those people we saw... I mean you said they looked like former cops but what if the cartel had guys in law enforcement?"

The more she expressed this theory out loud, the more holes she saw in it. Why would other cops kill her folks when they also saw the cartel as an issue? Unless they were corrupt? Her mind swirled with uncertainty. "Never mind."

The pack-raft self-inflated and Xander turned to face her. "I'm not ruling it out at all. I think you might be on to something. When I called in the first time, Lee mentioned our descriptions had already been given to the cops and they were pretty darned accurate. I'm not sure someone watching from a window would have been that good."

"So the cartel gave our information to the cops," she said out loud. She didn't like the sound of that. "Do you think that's what Aaron found out?"

"Possibly. That would mean that he'd be in real danger. Maybe they aren't sure he has what he mentioned having."

"The actual names?"

"Yeah. And other details. Names from a prisoner aren't enough—he needs evidence."

She wasn't surprised to hear that. "Maybe the encrypted files have it."

"Maybe. I can try another call to Van and see where the team is. I wouldn't mind a pickup out of the swamp," he said.

"Yeah, me too," she agreed. He moved away to make his call and she took her phone out of the dry-bag, putting her SIM in so she could check for missed calls and emails. She had two voice mails, which she listened to. One was a hang-up from an unknown number. The second was from Crispin Tallman's office warning her to be cautious and to go to the nearest police station for her own protection. A shiver went down her spine. Maybe it was just her imagination, but she wasn't as reassured hearing from the DA's office this time. The message's tone was measured but unsettling.

She disconnected the call as Xander walked back to her side.

"What are you doing?"

"Checking voice mails and then emails. I have to let Hilda know I'll be out again today," she said. "Tallman's office warned me to be careful who I trust and go to the cops for my own safety."

"We can discuss it after you take the SIM card out of your phone again. I want to limit the time you are on it."

"Why?" she asked as she texted Hilda she wasn't going to be in the office. Hilda immediately messaged back asking if she was okay.

Yes. Hope to be back to work tomorrow. Watch out for yourself and the staff. Aaron was into some dangerous stuff.

Thanks for the warning. We will. Stay safe. Xoxox

She hearted Hilda's last message and then turned her phone off and removed the SIM. She turned to Xander, who looked relieved as she put both items back into the drybag. "Did your team have any info for you?"

"First tell me what the district attorney's office said. Also, did you call them back?" he asked.

"No, just listened to the voice mail. They just said that I was in danger and to go to the cops so they could keep me safe," she said. "It wasn't Crispin but one of his assistants."

"Okay. Well, that fits a little bit with what Van told me. He hasn't been able to speak to Tallman at all. His office has strongly suggested that I turn myself in and bring you to safety. Van says as of right now they haven't been able to crack the encrypted files. But they are hopeful it will be by the end of day."

"We could just go to the jail and ask Aaron to open it," Obie said.

"Yeah, I'm pretty sure he'd tell them to *f* themselves."

"Maybe. I warned Hilda."

"I also asked Van to send someone over and he's sending Luna and Rick. They'll keep your coworkers safe and be on alert if anyone shows up there," Xander said.

Well, that seemed like a lot of good information. Why didn't that make her feel any better? Probably because they still didn't know what exactly was going on.

"I wish I understood this," she said.

"Me too. There is definitely more to this than Aaron let on when he contacted me and asked for a favor. I'm not sure if he is part of it or just stumbled on to it."

"What *it*?"

"Law enforcement. I think you're right about that. The way the information about us has been disseminated so quickly. The fact that the photos we saw were clearly surveillance photos. I think we've only scratched the surface of the danger that Aaron is in and that we are now involved in too."

Rowing across West Lake wasn't bad. It was hotter than it had been the day before, and Obie was quieter today. She was still trying to figure out things that she might have missed when she'd been younger, before her parents had died.

He wanted to help her, and he really needed the distraction. Their safety was still uncertain, especially while the identity of who was working for the cartel, and how far they were willing to go to silence Obie and him, remained obscured. "Tell me more about what you remember before your parents died. Was there anyone new hanging around?"

She continued to row, but her hands tightened on the oar.

"I was so busy with school that I wasn't really paying attention," she said. "Officer Wade was coming to our house a lot more and he and Daddy would close the door to the study to talk."

He was surprised to hear they had a study. "I guess I shouldn't have, but I assumed you lived in a more bare-bones house in the swamp. This area isn't known for having that kind of luxury."

"Ha. Mama had standards and Daddy built her dream home on the land they bought. It's cheap to live where others only see trouble. It abutted the swamp and spread out for acres behind the house. But it was large, made of wood and glass."

Some of the tension that was almost always present in her dissipated when she spoke that home. He knew she was going through rooms in her mind because that was what he did when he let his thoughts drift back to his own childhood. He could clearly remember the room he'd shared with Aaron, the twin beds on either side of the room, the student desks at the end of their beds and the walls covered in posters.

Both of them had been huge comic book fans and gamers. So whenever an anticipated game was released, they'd go down and buy the posters and put them up. He had stopped gaming for years because it was so closely tied to his brothers. But Kenji played Halo and had challenged Xander to try to best him. So he had started playing again.

He shook off those thoughts and forced his mind back to the puzzle he wanted to solve. "Who was Officer Wade?"

"I'm not sure. He wasn't a deputy at the sheriff's

office because they were all called deputy. Daddy just introduced him and said they were working together."

Interesting. So law enforcement but not local. "You made the connection to the cartel. Was that because you heard your father mention it?"

"Oh yeah, and he and Mama had a fight about them. She said something like 'La Familia Sanchez cartel is going to cost you your own family. Let it be.'"

She'd slipped into a deep Southern accent when she'd spoke her mother's words. "What did your father say?"

"Be easy. He used to do that all the time. Tell us to breathe and that everything would be okay," she said, her tone tightening again. "Guess he was wrong that time."

Maybe. So the mom was worried and there was a new "cop" at her house all the time. He wished she'd been older so she might remember more. It wasn't a lot to go on, but it was enough to prove that he needed to dig deeper. When they stopped for another break he was going to have Lee dig into Officer Wade.

"Did you ever hear Wade's first name?" he asked.

"No. I think Gator knew it. He kept in touch with Wade for a few months after we moved to Aunt Karen's. We both thought that it wasn't an accident. There was no way Daddy would have taken the airboat out without a thorough check and he would have noticed the small hole in the intake pipe."

"That was the cause? What happened exactly?"

"There was a spark from the engine and the fan on the airport flamed it and the boat caught on fire. The report said it was instantaneous and there was not time for Mama and Daddy to jump overboard."

Her tone implied she wasn't buying that either. "What do you think?"

"That they were killed and then someone made it look like an accident. Gator thought Daddy had evidence that involved officers who worked for him and the cartel. But no one was listening to two teenage kids even if they had respected our daddy."

"So then you got sent to live with your aunt, your bother kept in touch with Wade and then what happened to him?"

She pulled her oar out of the water and leaned forward. "He left. It was two weeks before his eighteenth birthday. So the cops and Aunt Karen looked for him for a little while but then he was an adult so they stopped."

"What about you?"

"I knew they wouldn't find him. Gator told me he'd had enough of Aunt Karen and he was going back to the swamp. He wanted me to go with him…but I said no."

"Do you wish you'd gone?" he asked. It had nothing to do with solving the puzzle of her parents' deaths but it would help him in the picture he was creating of Obie in his head.

She shrugged but didn't say anything.

There was something about looking into the past and almost wishing you would have made a different choice. But he was self-aware enough to realize he wouldn't have made different choices. He had the feeling that Obie was in the same place.

She might wish she'd gone with Gator, but she knew that she never would have. She chose to move forward with her life. That didn't mean she'd forgotten her parents, but she'd been strong enough to know that she couldn't go back. That there was nothing for her there.

He respected that. Hell, each new thing he learned about her made him like her more.

Until this moment, she had forgotten Officer Wade wasn't with the sheriff's office. Talking with Xander about the past continued to unlock these pieces of her memory. And the shoulders of the man she'd seen the back of in that photo with Aaron…could they be Officer Wade's?

But without knowing who he worked for, she felt like she was spinning her wheels. "Do you think Wade was talking to Aaron?"

"Perhaps."

She pulled her oar out of the water again and turned to face him, so frustrated. "Can you just give me a yes or no answer?"

"No," he said and for a moment she thought he might be teasing her. "I want to but we don't have enough information."

"I get it. When do you think we will?" she asked.

"We might have to go and talk to Aaron."

She had been wondering if that was the case. He was the one who'd dropped them in his mess and he was probably the only one who could figure it out. "He told me to take the card to the district attorney's office. I'm not going to ask if you think that means they might be working together. I'm pretty sure you'll say maybe."

"Perhaps," he said.

She shook her head, tempted to rock the raft and tip him into the lake. He was being so frustrating. But it was a distraction from the endless rowing and her thoughts bouncing between the present threat and the past. She wished she could remember more of those weeks from the time Officer Wade showed up until her parents had died. But she'd had a crush on a new boy and holed up in her room journaling. It had been the beginning of junior year and she hadn't been interested in her father's work.

"If it is Officer Wade and Aaron is in jail…maybe he's the one we should be looking into," she said.

"I agree. I'm going to ask my team to investigate him. Right now we are coming up with a lot of possibilities and any of them are viable but until we know more, they are just theories. I know you want answers. Heck, I would like them too. But for now getting you to safety is where the focus needs to be."

"Yeah, I get it. I mean I think we are doing everything we can to get safely to the marina."

"We are. And talking about different things that occur to us is a good exercise. It helps to see patterns the other one might not see. Like the one you made with Wade. That's a solid connection. Too bad you lost touch with him."

If she'd gone with Gator would she still have been in touch with Wade? Her life would have been very different, and more than likely she wouldn't be here in the swamp with Xander. Not meeting Xander… She wasn't sure she wanted that path, if that choice would have been better.

It felt pointless to be speculating. She just had to keep trying to figure out what Aaron's connection was to the cartel, and maybe to her parents.

Life didn't work that way. Aunt Karen had told her more than once that fair wasn't something that happened in life. Parents died, brothers ran away and girls had to just figure out how to take care of themselves.

Until this moment she didn't think she'd appreciated what Aunt Karen had given her. The woman had made Obie resilient and independent and as much as she might view her life as just an existence. She was safe and had a roof over her head. And usually no one was trying to kill her.

"Once we get to the marina, what's next?"

"I'm hoping my team will be there with transport. We can get to a safe house, clean up, view the data files and then make a plan."

"If that doesn't happen?"

"Then… I'll get us transport and to a safe house. Same plan except it's just you and me."

She preferred that option. She trusted Xander now but she wasn't sure about his team. She'd always had a very small circle of people around her. And she didn't know about bringing new faces into it.

It didn't matter what Xander wanted. If that SD card held information that his boss could use, who was to say that he wouldn't sacrifice Aaron to get it?

But as Xander said they didn't have to worry about that now. Right now it was just getting across the lake.

"Croc three o'clock," Xander said.

"That's a gator," she said, guessing it was a young adult. Looked to her to be about six feet long.

"Uh, what?"

"Yeah. Once we left the salt water behind we are in gator territory."

"Do they get along?"

"For the most part. They coexist down here. It's the only place in the world where that happens."

"The only place in the world," he repeated.

It made her think this might be the only place where she'd be comfortable with him. This time on the lake and on the run was starting to feel normal to her. Like this was her life from now on.

Her life with Xander? She knew that there wasn't a future in it but at this moment she couldn't imagine him not by her side.

Chapter 16

Storm clouds gathered behind them coming up from the Caribbean, and Xander started to steer them toward the northern shore line. West Lake was bigger than Cuthbert Lake, and though he'd thought they could make it across in a few hours, he had a feeling it was going to take much longer.

Obie was a champ, rowing and digging in stronger as the breeze kicked up and thick, warm raindrops randomly splattered on them.

"That storm isn't moving too fast, but it looks like it's a beast," she said. "This one… We might need to use the tent. Even then…we need to find some place that is sheltered."

"Yeah? I'll let you find that. I'll have to deflate the raft."

The rowed harder. Today he'd stayed more to the shoreline after the storm yesterday, so it only took them about ten minutes to get close enough so that Xander could jump out and pull them out of the water with one yank of his arm. Obie hopped out as soon as they were ashore and started scouting for an area.

This part of the lake was similar to the area near

Lake Cuthbert. There were cypress trees with their knobby knees sticking out of the water near the shore-line giving way to small bushes. The farther she moved from the lake, they encountered larger trees that she recognized as live oak and then one huge orchid tree.

As they got closer to the Everglades new flora and fauna were starting to show up. The area closest to the Atlantic was giving way to the inland swamp. The orchid tree's branches fell to the ground and while being under a tree during a lightning storm wasn't ideal, when she glanced back over her shoulder the wind and rain she could see moving across the lake toward them was fierce.

They might have a better chance under the tree's sheltering branches. She pushed under one in front of her and found that there was room enough for Xander's tent. She heard him following behind her.

"What do you think? It's a risk because of lightning but I don't know if we're going to find something better in the short time we have."

"Let's risk it. I'll pitch away from the trunk and branches," he said.

The area under the branches turned much darker. The storm was getting closer now. Xander pulled a flashlight out of his pack and then the tent. She noticed he'd deflated the pack-raft and just tossed it on the ground while he went to work on the tent. She pushed the pack-raft into his backpack and hefted it on one shoulder ready to get it in the tent once he had it up.

He had the stakes, and she dumped his pack on the

ground taking three from him. "Start pushing that one in. I'll lay the others out."

Last night she'd been too tired to help but today she wanted to pull her own weight. To show him that she was a partner and not a liability. She pulled the ground covering out and pushed the stake in as far as she could, moving on as Xander came up to secure it. Working together, they got the tent secured and up just as the wind swept through the branches bringing rain in on them.

"Get inside," Xander ordered.

She grabbed his pack as he unzipped and held the flap open for her. She pushed his pack in first and turned to take her flip-flops off before scooting backward into the tent. Xander followed a moment behind her. He zipped the opening closed as the wind and rain seemed to build around them.

They were dry for now, but who knew if they were safe or for how long.

Xander opened his pack and took out the blanket she'd used the night before, offering it to her. "Dry off with this."

She wiped her shoulders and legs and then handed it back to him. It might be harder to get back to civilization than she'd thought. The terrain was rough, and with people looking for them they couldn't take the paths and network of trails that would get them out of here with any speed.

"Do you think they mean for us to run out of food and maybe let the elements kill us?" she asked. "Don't say maybe. Just give me your best guess."

"I'm not sure that's the plan but it wouldn't hurt if

we disappeared with the SD card. They won't know we sent the files to Price Security."

No one knew except the two of them. The last day and a half had reminded her of pieces of herself she'd lost. And she knew that she didn't want to die here.

She wanted to get out of the swamp and figure out who Obie Keller really was. She'd thought she'd lost that swamp girl forever but now knew that she never could. It was part of her soul.

"I have some more protein bars," he said.

She opened her purse and dug around in it, hoping to find a candy bar that maybe she'd missed earlier or something. Anything that was tastier than the protein bars. She found a piece of mint gum that had fallen out of a pack. "I have a piece of gum we can split after."

He smiled over at her. "We might need to fish."

"After the rain worms come out and we can get some bait," she said, but she realized that he was pretty much saying they weren't making it to the marina today. She had figured that out too the moment she'd seen the big storm behind them. This was going to be one that lasted for a while.

The two of them were once again in the small tent together with a storm outside and she looked over at him. She tried to tell herself that she was only attracted to him because of the circumstances but that was a lie. She liked the man he was. The way he kept calm and even reluctantly revealed pieces of his past.

Being back in the tent with her was a kind of torture, and he wasn't sure he was going to be able to resist her this time. He knew that if he touched her, if he kissed her again, he wasn't going to be able to stop himself from making love to her. He wanted her and she wouldn't forgive him if he touched her and then pulled back again.

He wouldn't either.

He'd never been a wishy-washy man. That wasn't how he was built. And because he'd always prided himself on his iron control when he was with women, he falsely assumed that he wasn't one to fall. But that had ended today when they'd been hiding in the water watching the foursome clearly searching for them. He could no longer pretend that he didn't want her or that he could resist her. She'd somehow found her way under his skin.

"Should we high-card for the truth again?" she asked. "The only other game I know is Go Fish or Slap Jack."

"Slap Jack?"

"Oh, you don't know the high-skill game?" she asked.

He could tell she was teasing him and wondered what the game was she spoke of. He really didn't care because if he high-carded her for the truth, he was going to ask if she still wanted him or if she'd welcome a kiss from him. He had condoms in his pack because…well, he'd thought he might be out in Miami after he checked in on Aaron. But this wasn't a hookup.

Obie was no longer a stranger and that made everything inside of him tighten with both anticipation and a sort of fear. The last person he'd tried to protect that he cared for had been his brother. The one no one spoke about. The one who was now paralyzed.

But he'd found a kindred spirit in her that he hadn't expected to. One that made the blame he'd inflicted on himself seem less powerful.

"High card," he said, his voice low and gravelly. The lust that he wasn't bothering to temper or hide was there right below the surface.

She arched one eyebrow at him. "What truth are you after?"

"Have you forgiven me for yesterday and will you let me kiss you again?"

She shifted back from him, curling her legs underneath her as she watched him. "Depends."

"Is that your version of *maybe*."

"Perhaps."

This was her way of testing him. To take the temperature of his mood.

He was hotter than he'd ever been in his life and it had nothing do with the Florida heat or the swamp humidity. It came from Obie and he wasn't really in the mood to temper it or hide it from her.

"I want you, Obie. I'm not sure that's the best thing to admit to you but there it is. I know I was an ass last night so if you tell me to eff off I wouldn't blame you."

"And if I told you to eff me?"

Instantly his erection went rock-hard. His mind shifted, and any of the reasons he might have come up with to keep from having sex with Obie were gone.

He reached for her. But she put her hand on his chest. "I'm on the pill and don't have any STIs. What about you?"

"Clean bill of health and I'm not on the pill but I do have a condom in the backpack," he said.

"Would you use it?" she asked.

"Yes."

Of course he would.

He'd been watching her and she'd been slowly working her way under his skin. It wasn't just the way she looked, all feminine and fit. She was capable, and watching her in the swamp had been mesmerizing. She wasn't like any other woman he'd ever met.

He pulled the condom out of his bag and put it in his pocket before crawling over to her. She sat up straighter, then pushed her hair behind her ears like she was nervous. She licked her lips. He had no idea what to do to put her at ease, so he sat down next to her and pulled her against the side of his body. Her head fell to his shoulder, tipping backward to reveal the long line of her neck.

He ran his finger along it and watched as goose flesh spread down her neck and chest. He saw them spread down her arm as well. Her nipples tightened against the cotton fabric of his T-shirt and she shifted her shoulders, turning her head so that he felt the brush of her breath against his neck.

Her hand went to his chest as she turned toward him. He lowered his head, kissing her as he'd been wanting to do since the moment she'd come in his arms last night. He thrust his tongue deep into her mouth. Now that he had her in his arms he wasn't in a rush to get her naked. He took his time with the taste of her and the feel of her against his body.

Her hand was on his abdomen, her fingers kneading him through his own shirt. He put his hand on her breast cupping it and rubbing his palm against her erect nipple.

She gave a slight moan as she tipped her head farther back. Her neck was long and exposed. As he lowered his mouth, the scent of her was intensely arousing while he ran his lips along the column of her throat. She shifted closer to him; he pushed his hand up under the T-shirt at the back feeling the slender line of her spine.

She moved to straddle him but he wanted her underneath him. Wanted to be able to see all of her this time. He rolled her to her side and then to the ground. He shifted up on his knees as he undid the button on her shorts and then the zipper, pulling it down.

She lifted her hips and shimmied out of her shorts and panties, shoving them down her legs and then off. He undid his pants and freed his erection, taking out the condom and putting it on.

"Take your shirt off," she said.

He did, pulling it up and over his head and tossing it aside. She touched him. Her fingers burrowed through the light dusting of hair he had on his chest. She ran her finger around his nipple, which felt odd. He wasn't sure he liked it. But she moved on, her nails scraping down his side as she curled her fingers around his waist and urged him forward between her spread legs.

He took his time, running his hands up her legs. She'd gotten a few cuts and bruises as they'd made their way through the swamp and he lowered his head to kiss each of them. Taking his time to move up her legs from her ankles.

"I'm sorry you were hurt," he said.

She put her hand in his hair. Pulling his head up toward hers.

"I'm sorry you were too," she whispered against his lips. He tasted the passion in her kiss and felt it as her hips rubbed against his.

He'd seen her strength so many times so he was surprised by how small she felt. He kissed and caressed her, moving his hands down the side of her body and then teasingly circling her belly button before moving lower to touch her intimate flesh.

He ran his finger lightly over her clit and she dug her fingers into his shoulders as she pulled his mouth back to hers. Sucked his tongue deep into her mouth. "I want you inside me this time."

His cock jumped at her words and he shifted his touch lower to make sure she was ready for him. She was wet and ready and he pulled his hips back, positioning himself until the tip of his cock was at her entrance.

He sank slowly into her. Her body was tight and resisted him at first, but she dug her feet into the floor of the tent, pushing up toward him until he slid all the way into her. Hilt deep, he rested there. His body was tense and the need to thrust into her until he came rode him hard. But he wanted to make sure she enjoyed this too.

She had her hands in his hair again and arched against him, whispering sensual words in his ear. He stopped thinking about trying to control this and gave in to the power she had over him. He kept one hand on her clit teasing her until he heard her breath catch at the back of her throat and that groan he'd heard last night when she climaxed. He felt her pussy tightening around him and then he put his hand under her hip, lifting her up into his body as he thrust harder and faster into her. Driving himself higher and higher. Sensation spread down his back and his balls tightened before he came. He continued driving into her until he was empty and spent. He heard her groan again and then he collapsed against her, careful to support his weight. He rested his forehead against her and her eyes opened and she looked up at him.

She touched the side of his face with a gentle hand and he knew that he was never going to be able to go back to being just her bodyguard. Not that he'd been since the moment they'd entered the swamp. But he had at least been able to pretend to himself that he still held on to a bit of objectivity.

Now though he saw through that for the lie it was. There was no denying that he cared about her. He wanted to keep her safe and he would kill anyone who put her in harm's way.

The beast that he always kept tightly leashed inside had woken and was on alert now. There was no going back to the Xander that he'd been when Van had sent him to Miami.

He was the Xander Quentin who'd left the SAS and tried to fight the world. Before he hadn't had anything but rage and anger to fuel him.

Now, rather than those dark feelings born from his own guilt and shame, he had Obie and his desire to keep her safe.

"You okay?" he asked her.

"Yeah. That was nice. You?"

He hugged her close as he rolled to her back and she cuddled against his side. He knew he should get up and clean up. Get himself ready to defend her if anything happened, and given where they were and the people after them, that was a very real threat.

But he took these few minutes for the both of them. Just held her at his side and looked down at her. He'd never experienced anything like this before and knew he wouldn't again. He just held her and something like peace went through him.

Which scared him more than anything the cartel or the swamp could threaten him with.

He hoped he hadn't put her in jeopardy by making love to her but he couldn't regret it. Wouldn't let himself.

Chapter 17

"I'd like to know more about your family. I feel like I've told you about mine but there is a lot about you I don't know," she said, her voice soft and husky in the dark.

"What would you like to ask me?"

In the darkness of the tent it was somehow easier to open up. He'd cleaned up and they both were dressed again. He'd wedged his pack under his head and Obie was curled against his side as the rain continued to pound the tent. The wind was scary at moments, gusting and then calming down, but the storm seemed less fierce now.

"How did you and Aaron fall out?" she asked after they'd been lying together talking about her family.

He wasn't sure how to put into words what had happened. The story in his mind was full of emotion and action and, of course, a little blood. "You know I have three brothers. We were just always this rough little group. We fought and tried to best each other. Even when we played a sport, we played hard. The local A&E knew my mom by name because at least one of us was in there every few weeks needing stitching up or with broken bones."

"That sounds interesting. I can't imagine that kind of childhood. If I got hurt it was from brushing against a poisonous plant or stepping on something. Gator and I didn't fight."

"You are a woman," he said.

"Does that make a difference?"

"To me it does. I wouldn't just punch you," he said.

"You would Aaron?"

"Yes. In fact when we get out of this and I go visit him in jail I'm going have to try really hard not to deck him."

She laughed. "Well, don't. He is obviously in over his head, which is why he called you. He must know he can count on you."

"He can," Xander said. Even though they hadn't spoken and he'd been reluctant to come to Miami, he knew he wouldn't have been able to resist for long. That bond formed in blood, sweat and fistfights was too strong.

"See, that's good. So you grew up roughhousing with your brothers," she said gently.

"Yeah, I guess that's a better way to put it. When I was fifteen and Aaron was sixteen we were playing rugby at the local pitch. It was me and Tony versus Aaron and Abe. Do you know rugby?"

He was trying to avoid answering her. Setting up the story so that maybe she wouldn't see that he was the one responsible for everything that happened. That she wouldn't get a glimpse of the monster that he had been. That she'd still see whatever version she'd made him. Because she liked that guy and Xander had never truly been able to like himself after that rugby match.

"Sort of. Isn't it like football without pads?" she asked.

"Yeah, sort of. It's a rough game, sort of a test of strength and power. The game was really just another way for us to fight without really fighting. I hit Aaron hard in a tackle and he hit his head. There was blood."

"And he got mad after that?" she asked. She was running her fingers along the folds in his T-shirt, plucking them into peaks and then pushing them flat. Her touch was soothing and he could almost close his eyes and drift off.

Except that was a lie. Now that he'd let himself start remembering that day there was nothing soothing about it.

It had rained and the field was muddy. Tony high-fived him when he'd taken Aaron down hard. Aaron and Abe were huddled together and looking over at the both of them.

There was no way they'd allow a tackle that hard to go unanswered. But Tony was the biggest and strongest of the four of them, even if he was second oldest. He pulled Xander close and told him he'd take the hit.

Xander disagreed. He could handle Aaron, but Tony didn't argue. When the play started again he just shoved Xander to the side as Aaron tackled Tony hard to the ground.

None of them had paid attention to their position on the old pitch or that they'd drifted toward the side. They were too intent on winning, on beating the other team. When Tony hit the ground it was hard, and at first Xander thought his brother was just dazed. But Tony's neck had hit a large rock and he took damage to his spine and the higher cervical nerves, which left him paralyzed.

"It was all my fault," he said.

"How do you figure? Aaron hit your brother not you and I'm not blaming Aaron either. How could you have known that would happen?" Obie said.

He was surprised to realize he'd been talking out loud, that he was finally admitting the truth. "I knew Aaron would retaliate."

"Your brother did too. He protected you."

"Yeah. Well, that's the last time anyone did. I realized that day that I had to take care of myself."

She pushed herself up with her arm on his chest and looked down into his face. "Why?"

"Because it's easier to handle the pain of broken bones and skin."

The rest of that afternoon was a blur. He knew they'd called an ambulance and their mom. Aaron was in shock and denial. He ran away before the ambulance came. After that they were never the same. He didn't try to talk to anyone; that wasn't what Quentin men did.

He'd helped his brother as much as he could. But eventually seeing big, strong Tony not able to move on his own had broken something in Xander and he had to leave. "I joined the Royal Marines and got a chance to join the SAS. Aaron was chosen as well. We didn't touch each other but we competed in everything. I was determined to beat him and prove I was the better man. Not like that would change what had happened."

"That was the last time I saw him," he said.

"Was that why you were so reluctant to come and help?"

He sighed. "No. Not that."

"Then what?"

Obie's heart ached for Xander and how it had shaped him into the man he was today. It also explained why he hadn't just rushed to Aaron's side. A wedge had come between the two men. She was pretty sure he wasn't going to say any more for now.

She heard a familiar sound and sat up. "Airboat."

"What?"

"That's an airboat."

"Do you think they can find us?" he asked. Scrambling up and getting his weapon, he moved to the opening of the tent.

"The branches are offering some cover and we are on higher ground. The path was dry around us but with all the rain it might be wet enough for them. I don't know. I guess I should have led with that."

"It's good. Let's get out of the tent. We're pretty much sitting ducks here."

She put her cross-body bag on but left her flip-flops in it. She'd need to move quickly and was more sure-footed without them. She moved next to Xander by the tent flap. He started to lift the zipper when the engine of the airboat seemed to get closer and a spotlight moved through the branches of the trees.

Her heart was racing. As Xander had said, this tent wasn't going to offer any protection to them at all. He pushed his body in front of hers, using it to shield her as he opened the flap. She couldn't see anything but his big back and neck. The spotlight moved past them. Xander exited the tent and then offered her his hand. She scooted out and immediately moved back toward the large trunk of the tree. Using it as a shield, she made herself as small as possible. Xander pulled his pack out of the tent and then moved to Obie's position.

He handed her his weapon as he put the pack on. "Let's move away from here, but not too far. I want to get a look at them."

It was dark and hard to see so Obie made her way carefully out from under the orchid tree's sheltering branches. The ground was marshy but too dry for an airboat. She scanned the dark horizon and noticed a clump of some trees a short distance to the left. She had no idea if an animal or snake was already using the area and they wouldn't be able to check before they ducked into cover there.

She nudged Xander with her elbow and he looked at her, eyebrows raised. She pointed to the area and when he urged her to move she leaned closer to whisper in his ear, "There could be something in the bushes. Might be dangerous."

"Understood. I think it's a chance we have to take."

His low tone was confident as always, but she was scared. She was reaching the end of her resilience. There wasn't much more she could take.

Now she was worried about Xander too. Not that

she hadn't been at first, but he'd been a stranger and he definitely wasn't any longer.

She darted quickly across the clearing to the area she'd spotted and it was full of low trees and fallen branches. Not really much of a cover, but they could duck behind the fallen tree limbs and use them as a block from being seen.

Xander was right behind her. "Good job. Duck down so that your head isn't visible."

"How will I see them?" she asked.

"You won't. I will. Take my phone and open the message app and hit SOS and Send."

He shrugged out of the pack and set it between the two of them. She dug out his phone from the drybag, which was near the top. It was password protected.

"Password."

"Checkmate."

Of course it was. She typed it in and then found the message app. There was an SOS button right at the top so she hit it. She watched it send, wondering who he was calling. And why hadn't he done that earlier.

But she was pretty sure she knew why. They'd both been thinking they'd be at the marina hours ago. And whoever was searching for them was out in some really shitty weather trying to find them. They weren't giving up easily.

"Sent."

"Who did you call?"

"My team. I thought we'd be okay but there is something I'm missing if they are searching this hard for us," he said.

"I was wondering that too. I mean you said if we died—"

"Not just that but why not wait for us to come out of the swamp and hit us then?" he asked.

"I don't know."

"I don't either. Those encrypted files are the key. We need to get into them," Xander said.

She agreed, but if his team couldn't crack into them then the only solution was going to get Aaron to talk to him. But Aaron was in jail, so that meant…she'd have to contact Crispin Tallman's office and get him to talk to Aaron for them.

She knew that Xander trusted his team to come and help them. But they might not make it in time to save them from these people who weren't giving up.

Xander took his phone from her and put it back into the pack. She thought maybe the airboat had moved on but it doubled back. She held her breath as two men got off of it and walked to the orchid tree, finding their tent.

Obie was a good partner, staying low at his side. She'd done everything he asked, but he heard her quick intake of breath when the men started to search their tent. There was nothing left inside of it and they could make any guesses as to what they thought happened. He saw them looking for a trail and was tempted to stay put and let the guy find him so he could take care of things once and for all. But giving away their position might be more dangerous right now.

Obie wasn't a fighter and he wouldn't put her in danger. Instead he took her arm and pointed behind them.

She got low and crept forward on her stomach. His pack was big and would raise his profile and he needed to keep his hands on his weapon. He was tempted to leave it but anyone who found it would know who he was and be able to track him to Aaron.

He turned and noticed that Obie was waiting with her arms extended. She'd already figured out his pack was a problem. He pushed it as quietly as he could with one great shove toward her. She grabbed the straps and pulled it toward her body and into some deeper coverage.

They were out of the mangroves. The trees and ground cover here wasn't as bountiful. But Obie read the swamp and found them the best coverage she could.

He kept low, crawling to her spot and ducking into the brush next to her. "I'm not sure if we are going to be able to find more coverage than this."

Her whispered comment only reached his ears and he used his free hand on her shoulder to squeeze, hopefully reassuring her that it was okay. "I'll make this work. Stay hidden as long as you can. I'll take care of them."

He glanced at her to see if she understood. Her face was tight; she just gave him a small nod. The tension was palpable and he felt like he was failing her as a bodyguard. He never should have made love to her. He should have been paying attention to the elements and had them on the move before the airboat came.

But he'd wanted those few moments for himself. Had held Obie in his arms and felt like he was okay. But that had made things worse. Much worse.

The men searched in a pattern, but when they reached the fallen logs where he and Obie had first hid they scanned the landscape. One of them shrugged and then they turned back toward the airboat.

It might be a setup. Pretend that they were going to move on but stay close enough to keep an eye on their target. There was no getting back to the lake since the airboat was between them.

And the brush here wasn't dense enough to provide cover for the both of them. The SOS signal he'd had Obie send would give his location to Van. His boss would be on the way, but he might be leading the team into a firefight, or worse. He needed to get to a spot where he could provide better cover for them.

"We have to move."

"Do you think it could be a trap?" she whispered to him.

"Yes. So when we move assume they are watching us. I need to get to higher ground. My boss will respond to the SOS and I don't want to leave him open to attack."

"What should I do?" she asked.

"Stay with my pack. I think you're shielded for now. I'll watch you as well. But I can move quieter or more easily on my own."

Her lips tightened and her eyes got wide. He put her hand on his shoulder and then on the side of his face. "Stay safe. I don't want you to get hurt," she said.

"Don't worry about me," he said, though he appreciated that she was concerned for him. He was going to make damned sure they were both okay. No matter what it took.

He wished he'd packed a rifle because that would give him an advantage that his handgun didn't have.

"Stay hidden until I come back for you unless they find you. Then run in the direction I'm going and I'll cover you. Leave the pack and everything but the SD card. Okay?"

"Yes." Her voice quavered on the word. "I don't think you'll have to do that but better to be ready for it."

"Thanks," she said.

He leaned in and gave her a quick, hard kiss on the mouth and she hugged him tightly to her. He savored the embrace for a moment and then turned and made his way out of their hiding spot. He stayed low, watching the path in front of him while keeping his senses trained on the direction that the men had gone in the airboat.

Airboats were noisy, which was one thing in Xander's favor. But Xander feared they'd ditch the airboat and come back on foot. He listened until for the sound of the airboat and it seemed to be moving away from their position, but that didn't mean the threat had passed.

He kept moving until he found a copse of trees close enough together to offer him some cover. They weren't large but were big enough he should be able to stand up, which would give him a better view of anyone who came at Obie.

Chapter 18

Obie felt panic rising in her like tidal changes. Xander was no longer visible from her location. She didn't doubt that he was watching over her. But he was one man with a handgun and a knife. There were at least two men who had been looking around their campsite clearly aiming to capture them.

They were officially in over their heads.

The weather hadn't cooperated either. But the weather was the least of her problems. Like her daddy used to say, she wasn't going to melt from the rain. But she could die from a bullet.

She heard the airboat as it pulled away from their area and then moved off toward the east. From growing up in the swamp she knew that the sound could carry for a very long way, so when it disappeared about ten minutes later, she suspected that wasn't good news.

Had the men left to double back? Were they going to wait and see if she and Xander showed up?

An organization as big as the cartel had a lot of resources. They probably had a large number of people they could hire to search for her and Xander.

The storm had moved on but some rain and clouds

lingered, and it was close to sunset even though they couldn't see it.

If they were going to make it through the night they'd need help.

She looked at her hands, which were shaking, and then back across the swamp to where Xander had disappeared. Knowing what she had to do, and even if it was something he wouldn't agree with, she took her phone out of her purse and the drybag. She put the SIM card in.

As soon as it booted up, she realized it was almost dead and she had no signal.

Xander's pack was right there. She knew where his phone was. She'd just used it to send his SOS signal. She pulled his phone out. His signal was weak and the SOS hadn't gone through. Hell.

She hit the button to send it again. While it was slowly trying to connect she made the decision that she'd been debating for the last few minutes.

Getting the number from her phone for Crispin, she texted him from Xander's phone. Said they were being tracked by dangerous-looking men and were heading toward the marina at the west side of West Lake. She hit Send, not sure if either message would get out.

Then she put Xander's phone back in his pack and turned hers off since it was about to die didn't bother with the SIM card. There was no one around and the sounds of the swamp seemed muted. Or maybe that was simply the rising panic in her own ears.

She couldn't sit still much longer and put her cross-body bag on and then moved to put Xander's backpack on, too. When someone lifted it up, she screamed and turned as a hand came over her mouth.

The touch was familiar, and when she gazed up she saw it was Xander. "How? I just looked and didn't see you."

"I crawled. I think it's time to move," he said. "Sorry for the scare. How far do you think the airboat traveled before it stopped?"

She wasn't good with distance. "It's hard to tell in the swamp. It felt like about ten minutes until I could no longer hear them."

"Same. Let's move out. We'll stick to those trees over there," he said.

"Okay." She should tell him she'd sent the text to Crispin.

"Did the SOS send?"

"Not when I first hit it. I just tried sending it again. The storm was probably interfering before."

"Maybe. Either way I'm getting you to the marina tonight," he said.

She agreed. "*We* are getting out of here tonight. I want you safe too."

"I'm used to being in the line of fire."

"That doesn't mean that I like seeing you in it."

He leaned down and kissed her quick and hard like he had earlier. But didn't say another word. He put his backpack on and then held his hand out to her to help her to her feet. He put his hand on the small of her back and pushed her toward the tree line. She moved quickly, watching where she stepped because she was still barefoot.

Running in flip-flops wasn't an option, and until she knew that the men who'd been looking for them weren't behind them, she'd have to leave them off.

They walked along the trees for what seemed like hours until they got to the north side of the lake. Xander was very cautious keeping his eye on the trees, and now that it was twilight there were more shadows.

The sounds of the swamp had always been a lullaby to her but they weren't any longer. Because she didn't want to face another unexpected danger, didn't know what other sounds were hidden beneath.

Suddenly there were lights in the distance.

Xander grabbed her arm and pulled her down behind the large trunk of a live oak. She held her breath as he pulled out his weapon and they both waited.

Van walked into the clearing and Xander let out a sigh of relief. "That's my boss."

He pulled Obie to her feet and led her out into the open toward Van. As soon as they stepped out of the trees, he heard a bullet fly past his head. He pushed Obie behind him and turned to return fire, but men stepped out surrounding them.

Van put his hands in the air and Xander did the same. Obie was between the two of them. "We don't want any trouble."

"We just want the card." The man who stepped forward was one of the two who'd been in the airboat. He had a handgun held loosely by his side and wore a bulletproof vest over his T-shirt and camo pants.

"We don't have it," Xander said.

"We know you do," the man said. "That's why we've been looking for you."

He edged closer, and the other two people they'd seen with the men earlier in the day appeared out of the surrounding swamp as well. The other three were armed and looked dangerous.

Xander liked his odds a lot better with Van by his side.

"Let's keep calm," Van said, his voice low and gravelly but loud enough to be heard. Several people stepped out in to the clearing, all armed with AK-47s and wearing bulletproof vests.

"Give us the SD card," the man closest to them said.

"I already said we don't have anything," Xander said. He shrugged out of his backpack, letting it fall to the ground. There was no way they were getting out of here without a fight.

And that was fine with him. He wanted to know who these men were working for. The only way he was doing that was by getting information from one of these four.

"Then you're useless."

He turned back to the man who'd spoken and saw him lift his handgun and fire, taking aim not at Xander but at Obie. He spun quickly, putting Obie between himself and Van.

He lifted his own weapon and fired back, hitting the assailant in the shoulder, and the other man's gun dropped to the ground. Xander felt the burn of the shooter's bullet in his left side but ignored it, turning to return fire from the woman on his left.

He hit her in the shoulder and was preparing to fire again when he saw Rick Stone come up behind her and put his gun between her shoulder blades. "Drop it. This close, even a vest can't really protect you."

She dropped her weapon. He turned and noticed that Luna and Kenji were there as well. They disarmed the other two men and Van had subdued the guy that Xander had shot.

He turned to Obie, who was white as a ghost.

"I don't know how the hell they found us. I'm glad the team got here when they did," he said.

"I don't know either," she said. Her hands were shaking. "Are you okay?"

Glancing down at his aching side, he saw blood seeping through his T-shirt. The bullet had only grazed him but had burned though his shirt and skin. He pulled the fabric away and knew he'd need some first aid.

But so would two of the people who'd attacked them. Van took charge. "Rick, you have medic training—see to the wounded. Kenji, get those other two over here. I want to ask some questions. X, you want in on the questioning?"

"You know I do."

"His wound needs to be cleaned first. This is the swamp not some sterile environment," Obie said.

"Of course. I'm Giovanni Price," he said, holding his hand out toward Obie.

"Obie Keller," she said, taking his hand.

"Nice to meet you."

Van turned away and walked toward Kenji to start talking to the men who'd attacked them. Rick stayed with the woman who'd taken a hit in her shoulder and Luna was working on the guy who'd been hit as well.

Obie went to get first aid supplies from Rick and then came back. "That was dangerous what you did. Why did you do that?"

"What was my option, let him shoot you while I stood there?" he asked her.

"No, I guess not. But I don't like seeing you shot."

"Trust me, this is nothing. I'm not bigging myself up and being all butch. It's just that his aim was bad and the bullet barely grazed me."

"You're bleeding," she pointed out.

"It was a slight hit."

He pulled his T-shirt up and off the wound, cursing as the fabric pulled away from it. She gingerly touched it, cleaning the wound before putting a bandage on it. "That will do for now. So are all these people on your team?"

"They are. I'm glad they got here when they did."

"Me too. Do you think those men were following us?" she asked him.

"I know you're not a fan of this answer but maybe. The part that has me not sure is the guy who came from the same direction as Van."

"Do you think they followed your boss?" she asked.

"No. They definitely didn't follow him," he said.

"Then how would they know where we were? Unless…? I turned my phone on."

He looked over at her. "When?"

"After the airboat left. I wanted to call Crispin. You're strong and everything but still just one man."

"Did you call him?" he asked.

"My phone didn't have a signal," she said, chewing her lip between her teeth. "I used yours to text him. I told him we were heading to the marina."

Xander turned and stalked away from her. So angry at the moment he wasn't sure he could control his temper. If she had trusted him she wouldn't have put them in this position. Or was he making a jump to judgment? Maybe it wasn't Crispin who had alerted the men who followed them. Soon they'd find out.

But until then he needed some distance.

Obie moved closer to Giovanni, though she heard the others calling him Van as he was questioning the men. She noticed the gang tattoo that they'd seen on the first day on their attackers.

Xander had disappeared into the trees and she wasn't sure what to do.

Van finished questioning the men who were tight-lipped, then he called a contact in the DEA, who came and arrested the four people. Xander still wasn't talking to her as they all got into the chopper that Van and his team had arrived in. It was some big military-looking one, and they all flew back to Miami, landing at a private gated beachfront house.

It was a shock to her system to step out of the helicopter and feel soft grass under her feet and not the roughness of the swamp.

Xander started to brush past her but she grabbed his arm. "We need to talk."

"I can't. I'm still mad."

She shook her head. "Fine, then just listen."

He took a deep breath as his team moved past them. She led the way to a pool, which was well lit and had chairs positioned around it. She sat down because she was tired and Xander stood there, glowering at her for a minute before she pointed to the chair next to her and he sat down.

"I'm sorry I didn't do what you asked. I was worried for your safety. You are big and capable and you definitely know your stuff and can keep me safe. But there were four of them and only one of you."

He looked like he was going to speak but she put her hand up to stop him. "I'm not sure if they just surrounded us or if they got the information another way but when we were alone in the swamp I felt there was nothing else I could do to actually help other than to call and ask for it."

Xander leaned back in the chair, stretching his legs out in front of him. He had to be as tired as she was. Every part of her ached and she wanted a shower and some food and to never see these shorts or top again. But it was more important to her to set things right with Xander.

It had only been the two of them for what felt like a lifetime, and now that they were back in Miami everything would change. She didn't want to let him leave thinking that she hadn't trusted him to protect her.

She cared deeply for him, and it was only when she'd seen him put himself between her and a bullet that she'd realized *how* deeply.

"I get it. There is nothing that I could have said to make you feel safe—"

"I felt safe, but you proved to me my worst fears. You weren't safe. You would put your life on the line for me, Xander. That's something that I… I just didn't want you to do."

She licked her lips. They were sunburned and chapped and she was tired and wanted something she wasn't sure she'd be able to have. To just crawl into his arms in a real bed and sleep, knowing they were both safe.

"The last person to try to protect me was Tony," he said.

"I know."

She reached out for him and he let her touch him. She put her hand on his arm and squeezed. "Maybe it's time you let someone else do it. I'm fine."

"For now. And it was a near thing. If that bullet had hit you it would have been low in your stomach."

He sat forward and took her face in his hands. "I can't stop thinking about how close he came to killing you. You are under my protection and those men got the jump on us. I wish you hadn't called the district attorney but the truth is I'm not sure he's connected to those guys. No one is. But I do know that I almost let you get injured."

"Almost? You didn't let anything happen to me," she reminded him, shifting forward until she could brush her lips against his. "You kept me safe."

He didn't say anything else, just lifted her out of her chair and onto his lap, holding her tightly, his head buried in her hair. "I would die before I let anything happen to you, Obie."

They held each other for a few more minutes. Then went up to the house to get cleaned up. Van and his team had spare clothes for them. She showered and got dressed and then went out on the patio where Van was at the grill cooking for the team. There was an ice bucket with Coronas in it and music playing from the speakers. It was so normal it was strange.

She looked around for Xander but didn't see him.

"I'm Luna," the woman said. She had long brown hair that she wore pulled back in a ponytail. She had on a pair of khaki shorts and a light green T-shirt.

"Obie. Thanks for coming to get us."

"No problem. How was the big guy in the swamp?" Luna asked. "He hates the heat."

"He was good. He just kept focused on moving us toward the marina. He's really good at adapting."

"Yes, he is. He's done it often enough," Luna said.

Xander came out a minute later and everyone moved to sit at the table. Obie didn't pay too much attention to what was going on around her at first since this was the first meal she'd had in day or more. But then she noticed that Xander seemed to really fit in with this group. The laughed and joked and talked quietly between each other. He made more sense here with these other highly skilled bodyguards than anywhere else she'd seen him. Which didn't bode well for the way she felt about him.

Chapter 19

Lee came onto the patio looking tired and like she hadn't slept in twenty-four hours. "Broke the encryption. Whoever did the coding was really good. And you guys are not going to believe what's on there."

Xander looked over at Obie, who reached for his hand. He squeezed hers and instantly she saw he was worried. But not knowing was worse than whatever was in those files.

"What have you found?"

"Well, that guy from the district attorney's office that you had me contact…seems like he's close with La Familia Sanchez. Like his cousin is the head of the cartel. Your brother stumbled onto some really sensitive information and put it all together," Lee said.

She connected her laptop to the TV on the patio and streamed the information to it. There were the documents, which, as soon as he read the first line, he knew that Aaron had written. The way he strung words together was distinct and it almost sounded like his brother was talking to them.

Lee read the documents aloud:

"The Sanchez crime family has deep connections not just in south Florida but throughout the entire country. Ten years ago Bartolo Sanchez was just a lieutenant in the cartel but made a big move to spread the operation out of south Dade County. The move was profitable, but what really made the move work was Bartolo's idea to have members of the gang take jobs within law enforcement and the criminal justice system.

"Working with DEA officers, I have been able to find some connections throughout Florida. I've passed the positions and the profile types of these men and women on to my counterparts working the operation in other parts of the country.

"In Miami I have gathered circumstantial evidence pointing to Crispin Tallman, who is married to Bartolo's cousin Luisa. However I'm pretty sure my cover was blown when I made contact with my handler two weeks ago. The photos are included on this card. I suspect I'll be arrested. In which case I will reach out to a civilian who I trust to retrieve the card and crack the encryption."

Lee stopped reading then and looked over at him. "I assume he means you."

"Yeah. Does the rest of the file have the evidence?"

"It does. Seems that someone on Aaron's team made sure that his case went to Tallman so that he could mention the evidence," Lee said.

"He was probably hoping that Tallman would go after me knowing I could handle the heat," Xander said. And because he'd hesitated, Aaron had no choice but to send Obie after the SD card. He had to retrieve it so that Tallman would show his hand.

"Why didn't he protect Obie after he sent her in?" Xander asked. He understood that some plans couldn't be stopped once they were in motion, but Obie had no training and if Xander hadn't been at Aaron's house he was pretty sure she would have been killed and the card would have been taken by Tallman's men.

"He did," Van said. "I had a call from the Aaron in jail as well. Your brother told me he needed you for a job. That's why I insisted."

"Did he give you any details?"

"No, just said it was a family thing," Van said. "I didn't push because you are tight-lipped about your family. I knew that you weren't going to want to go but he was insistent you were the only man for the job."

Aaron hadn't been wrong. Obie needed protection and the first moment, he'd do anything to keep her safe. He would have done the same thing for anyone that his brother sent into danger.

"Why didn't you mention this before?"

"I told you to go and I knew you wouldn't disobey an order no matter how much you might resent me for forcing you to leave. Saying your brother had called me wasn't going to help matters," Van said.

"Fair enough. I guess he had Obie call me because he thought I'd say yes to her," Xander said.

"I really don't like that Aaron used me," Obie said.

Lee pulled up another file. "I'm sure he wanted to keep you out of it, but if you read this file you'll see why he thought you were the best person for the job."

Xander's eyes went to the screen as did everyone else's.

Bartolo's big move that had gotten him promoted was infiltrating the sheriff's department in central Florida. The file went on to detail how DEA Agent Wade had been contacted by Sheriff Keller and, once arriving, had found that his suspicion that drugs were being run through the swamps on airboats was accurate. They started their investigation and noticed that two officers—Deputy Lawrence and Deputy Peters—were always on duty when the airboat activity was reported by locals. Both deputies reported nothing to be alarmed about and that the increased airboat activity was down to better fishing in the swamp thanks to extra rains.

Sheriff Keller and his wife started to do extra patrols from their home and Officer Wade's report said that he believed the sheriff and his wife must have witnessed criminal activity and confronted the cartel members when they were killed and it was made to look like an accident.

Officer Wade saw Deputy Peters the next day and the man had claw marks from what appeared to be a human hand on his face and neck and a busted nose.

Obie started crying softly next to him and he pulled her into his arms, hugging her close. She and her brother had long suspected that the cartel was involved in their parents' deaths but this proof had to be hard to take.

She just kept her head in his chest and Lee closed the file and opened the photos, which showed two men that Xander didn't recognize. "Let's take a few minutes before we figure out what to do next."

Obie couldn't help but think of those marks on the deputy's face, imagining her mom in some kind of fight with the man. Her mama was tough and fierce, so Obie wasn't surprised she'd fought the man who had killed her and Daddy. In her heart she'd always known that there was more to it than an accident but she wasn't really sure knowing the truth helped at all with her grief.

It made her mad as hell to think of men who worked for her father betraying him.

Everyone went to take the break that Xander had suggested. Only the two of them remained on the patio.

She lifted her head from his shoulder and wiped her eyes. Later she knew she would go over the details of what had happened, but right now she wanted justice for her parents, and payback.

"How are we going to get Tallman and Bartolo Sanchez?" she asked Xander.

"Straight to that, well okay. The team will come up with a plan and then we will put it into motion."

"I want to be part of it. I'm not letting them get away with killing my parents or with almost killing you and me," she said.

"We won't."

Xander didn't seem to be hearing her, which was very frustrating. She got that he wanted to protect her. He'd done his job well. But they were back in the city and she was the one with the connection, as weak as it was, to Tallman.

"I'm not sitting this one out, Xander. I want to catch him. It's men like him that made sure that Deputy Peters didn't even have a comment on his record after his involvement with my parents' deaths. He was at their funeral."

Her voice cracked and she shook her head, refusing to let her emotions get the better of her. Not now. Later when Tallman was behind bars and Bartolo Sanchez had been arrested.

"I understand. But—"

She shook her head and interrupted him. "No, you don't. That man sent killers to find me knowing I'd be at Aaron's house in Key Largo by myself. He didn't send just one person—there were like what, six? That's overkill. I can't let you do this alone. You look just like those former law enforcement guys who your team captured and like Aaron. You can't go in and talk to him. He'll immediately suspect you and clam up."

Xander pushed to his feet and walked a few feet from her, turning his back toward her and putting his hands on his hips.

"It can't be me," he said at last. "But it doesn't have to be you either. There are other ways to catch him."

Obie got to her feet and walked over to him. Putting her hand on the small of his back, she leaned around to look up at him. "There are other ways, but I have to be involved in this. I want to take him down. To show him he underestimated me."

He sighed and then put his arm around her, pulling her close to him. Lowering his head, she felt the ragged exhalation of his breath against her neck. "I can't let you get hurt."

She hugged him tightly back to her. She didn't want to see him get hurt either. Over the last forty-eight hours she'd fallen hard for this big British bodyguard who was so careful about letting anyone know who he truly was. But she'd seen him from the beginning. Maybe because of her connection to his brother or her own relationship with Gator.

Something about Xander had drawn her to him the first second she'd seen him. And the last two days had put them in a pressure cooker. A place where there was no time for the facade that she usually kept in place. They'd been stripped raw. Her feelings for him were real and would last for a long time.

She had no idea if he'd stay or if they'd end up making a life together. But her love for him was real. She wanted to tell him, but that seemed secondary to getting his agreement that she could be the bait to set up Tallman and get the evidence they needed for his arrest.

"I'm not going to back down on this. Your boss is smart and once I point out that I'm the logical choice he'll agree. And the only way I can do what is needed is if I know you have my back and are watching over me."

He gave another ragged sigh. "You know I will be. I won't let anything harm you."

His words were firm, sincere and she took them as the promise she knew he meant them to be. She put her hands on his dear face. He'd shaved when they got back, making his cheeks smooth after the stubble that had been there for the last few days. She leaned up and kissed him. Taking her time, hoping that he'd understand from this embrace just how much he meant to her, and that as much as he wouldn't let anything happen to her, she was going to do her best to keep him safe as well.

The information Lee had shared with them would have struck Xander just as deeply as it did her. He was protective of his brother, as much as he said he didn't know the man anymore. He would want to take down the man who was putting his brother in danger. Xander had told her he turned into a beast when someone he loved was threatened and she believed him.

She didn't want him to have to do that. It would be violent and there was a chance that Xander could end up getting himself put behind bars. The only way to save the man she loved was to put herself in the company of a man who'd had no qualms about sending her to her death.

Xander wasn't sure he was going to be able to allow Obie to put herself in danger. She wasn't wrong about Van. He'd definitely see the plus in using Obie to get Tallman. Xander was also very sure his boss would keep Obie safe. The part that was troubling him was if he could keep himself under control.

Obviously they were both still tired from the last

two days in the swamp, so his control was hanging on by a thread. But added to that was the fact that he loved her.

She was like the swamp that they'd just traveled through. There were parts of her that were beautiful and breathtaking and parts that were dangerous, which he adored. She'd been so city girl when they first met, and he hadn't been sure she'd be able to cope with being shot at, but she'd handled it all like a champ.

She'd dealt with her fears and emotions honestly, which he couldn't help but respect. But she also made him feel safe in sharing his with her. He hadn't talked about Tony's accident or his brothers since the day it occurred. His mom hadn't been able to talk to any of them, and his father emoted by working more hours and being sullen at home.

Obie was the first one to make him feel okay that he was sad and angry about what happened. She had just listened and hadn't judged, which was something he hadn't realized he'd needed.

He loved her.

He'd known that last night when he'd held her in his arms instead of sitting at the tent flap with his firearm ready to defend her.

They'd forged a bond in the tent while that crazy summer storm roared outside and kept them safely from being found. Those hours together had been what they'd both needed.

A chance to find the human in each other.

He lifted his head and looked down into her big

brown eyes and knew that he wasn't going to be able to keep his feelings to himself. He put his hand on her shoulder, his thumb rubbing against her collarbone, and she tipped her head to the side.

"What?"

"I—"

"Gather up, team. It's time to make a plan," Van called as he came back on the patio.

Xander just nodded. "Later."

His feelings weren't going to change, and once Tallman was captured there would be plenty of time with Obie.

She slipped her hand into his as they walked back to the table. He noticed Van looking at their joined hands and then back to him, raising both eyebrows. Xander just smiled at the other man. She wasn't a paying customer; there was no rule that said he couldn't be with her. And if Van had a problem… Well, Xander wouldn't like it, but he was willing to walk away to have Obie by his side.

Van just smiled and nodded his head a few times.

"All right, so we need to get Tallman to confess to either setting Obie up or to being a part of the cartel. Ideas?"

Obie raised her hand and then sort of realized what she'd done and put it back down. "I think I might be the one to get him to confess. He set me up."

"He definitely did. What are your thoughts?" Van asked.

"She wants to go and confront him with the SD card," Xander said. "I'll keep lookout—"

"I'll help provide cover to," Kenji said. "I think Obie is the right choice. She knows Tallman and he definitely will be expecting her to make contact now that she's out of the swamp."

Xander knew that the DEA agent who'd arrested the people hired by the cartel was going to keep it under wraps for twenty-four hours. They were also interrogating the people to see if they could get a confession that would connect them to the cartel. But the cartel killed snitches so Xander was pretty sure that wasn't going to happen.

"Exactly. I'll go to my apartment and then call him from there. Might be best if Xander drops me off in case anyone is watching it," Obie said.

She had sound reasoning and, as she had in the swamp, was outlining a logical next step.

"I've been working at the coffee shop so I can show up at your place and act as a bodyguard in the apartment. I'm not sure he'll come for you there but that way you're not alone," Luna said.

"You'll have to wear a wire," Van said. "I guess we should get you to your apartment and make the call. Then see what Tallman suggests. Obie, if at any point you want to back out, just say and we will find another way to get him."

Even before she spoke, Xander knew that she wasn't going to back down. That wasn't her way. Obie was in this until Tallman was caught. He suspected it was a little bit about her parents' deaths and bringing some closure to her past as well as making up for not going with her brother. She tied those two incidents together the way he did his estrangement with Aaron to Tony's accident.

Both of them needed to take Tallman down to save their brothers and make some kind of peace with their pasts.

Chapter 20

It had been weird being back in her apartment after the last few days. She'd gotten dressed in her own clothes and that had felt nice. After a call to Crispin Tallman's office, he offered to meet her in a nearby park instead of having her come all the way downtown.

Assuming that the apartment building was being watched, Luna was the only one with her. Obie missed having Xander by her side but Luna was friendly and put her at ease.

"Let's get the wiretap turned on and then we can head out," Luna said. "Xander and Kenji are in position as snipers and honestly those two won't let anyone harm you. I'll go with you and then get out to jog while you go meet Tallman but I'll keep an eye on you as well. Rick's with the DEA agent monitoring the wiretap. As soon as they have enough to evidence to convict they'll come out and arrest Tallman. Lee will be monitoring everything and the smartwatch we gave you will only buzz if you need to duck and run."

They'd gone over the plan earlier and she knew that Luna was just running over it one more time reassure her there was nothing to worry about. "Is the tap on yet?"

Luna shook her head. "I'm about to turn it on. Why?"

"I'm scared. But I don't want Xander to hear that."

Luna gave her a reassuring smile. "That's normal. Fear will keep you alert and on your toes. You've faced tougher in the swamp. After hearing about the crocodiles you encountered I know that Tallman will be a piece of cake for you. But if you want to back out I can take your place. We are about the same height and I can wear large frames to disguise the differences in our faces."

Obie knew that Luna would do that. It was another thing they had discussed. And talking about her fear made her feel better. "I still want to do it but had to say it out loud."

"I get it. My husband was in danger when a madman had taken his father hostage and I was so scared for him because I knew he'd do anything to keep his father safe. It's hard to face that kind of fear but the truth is it made it easier for me to focus. I knew I had to keep Nick safe. That was it. I just focused on him and my fears faded."

"Thanks. It's hard for me to believe that you were ever scared," Obie said. The other woman was clearly well trained and she'd heard the stuff that Luna had done to keep her husband—a former client—safe. She knew that Luna had skills.

"I was. And my husband isn't a cautious man, he's always doing reckless things. Keeps me on my toes," Luna said.

"Sounds interesting."

"That's one way of describing him."

"I'm ready now," Obie said.

Luna turned on the wiretap and then they tested and got the affirmative that Rick was receiving the signal. He and the DEA agent were in a van nearby and would drive toward the public parking lot near the park where she was meeting Tallman.

All that was left to do was go and meet him. She had a blank SD card that she'd give to Tallman—they weren't going to risk giving him the one with the evidence on it. Xander and his team agreed that Tallman probably wouldn't check it at the meeting.

She looked around her apartment, decorated in that boho chic style that had been so popular and was on all the shelves at Target. It no longer suited her. She didn't want to be like everyone else anymore. She was tired of blending in. It was definitely time for her to step out of the shadow of the woman that Aunt Karen had made her.

Once this was over and Tallman was arrested, Obie was going to be make a new plan for her life. One that she hoped would involve Xander.

"Let's go."

Luna just smiled and followed her out of her apartment. The cross-body bag that Obie had used during the two days in the swamp was ruined and she was carrying a bag that Price Security had given her. There was a pouch in it that concealed a small derringer pistol as well as a tracking device and backup recording unit. They weren't taking any chances with her safety.

They walked out of the apartment building and the heat of the day wrapped around her. She'd left her hair curly today instead of straightening it like she used to for work.

She had tennis shoes and socks that made her feet sweat but she wasn't ready to leave her house in flip-flops. Not yet.

Her car was had been brought back to her place by a tow truck that Van had arranged. And waited in her normal spot. She unlocked the doors and realized that she wasn't as nervous now that she was on her way to meet Tallman as she'd been upstairs.

She remembered the way he'd sent her to that house to find the information that Aaron had hidden and to be killed so he could have it. That thought stiffened her spine and her resolve. She'd get him to confess no matter what it took.

She drove to the park and as soon as she turned off the car and got out, she knew there was no going back. She waved goodbye to Luna, who took off for her "run" and then looked around to see if Tallman was there yet.

She noticed a man sitting on a bench reading a paper and drinking coffee. Near the swings sitting on a blanket on the ground sharing a box of doughnuts was a mother and her young son. But that was all.

She didn't see him but started walking toward the picnic tables they'd agreed to meet at. The park was quiet at this time of day when commuters were heading to work and parents taking their kids to school.

* * *

Xander checked the sniper rifle that he'd brought with him, but as soon as they saw the setup of the park it was clear that two snipers weren't needed. Kenji was definitely better prepared than he was. "I'll go and get set up. You going to be okay with me on overwatch?"

"You're the best there is, so of course."

"Yeah, I am. But Obie… This is personal for you, Xan," Kenji said. "Not sure how I'd play this. I'd want to watch over her and still be close by."

"Lucky for me I can do both with you. I trust you more than anyone else, Kenji," Xander said.

Kenji nodded and pulled out a pair of glasses that he wore when shooter and then nodded. "That goes both ways."

They bro hugged and Kenji left. Xander looked for cover. He was too big to just chill on a park bench without drawing attention. He was pretty sure Tallman had his description since it had been sent to the police. Both himself and Obie were scheduled to talk to the local sheriff that afternoon. But for now it would be better for Xander to stay out of Tallman's sight.

The path that led to the tables was well landscaped with large palm trees and hibiscus bushes. After the heavy rains of the last few days, there were branches and leaves on the ground. Van had suggested that they appear to be part of the landscaping crew in the park.

Van had several disguises for the team depending on where Tallman suggested they meet. Xander was zipped into work overalls and had on a baseball cap and sunglasses. He was wearing a blond wig so that

"Got him. X, move in three, two, one."

Xander followed his boss's orders and moved from the trees he'd cleared, closer to the picnic tables. Obie was sitting on the table, not on the bench. She had the bag that they'd given her next to her.

He'd have to hope she kept it close in case she needed to protect herself. When he walked past he didn't look directly at her, but out of his peripherals he noticed her shrug the bag over her body as Tallman approached.

Xander dropped to his knees close to Obie's location and started to pull debris from the flower bed nearest her.

"Ms. Keller. It's good to see you. I was getting worried about you," Tallman said.

"I was getting worried too. It was so scary when those men were shooting at me. I didn't think anyone knew I'd be at Aaron's house," Obie said.

Xander held his breath hoping she wasn't being too obvious.

"I guess trusting Quentin was a dangerous thing to do. He definitely has enemies," Tallman said. "Was the information where he said it would be?"

Xander turned as if reaching for the bag that he'd brought over with him and shoved the branches slowly into it as he continued watching Obie.

"Yes. But I'm not sure it's going to be useful. It looks like a memory card," she said. "Not sure what kind of reader it works in."

"I'm sure the people who work for me will figure it out," he said. "Let me see it."

"Shouldn't I give it to Aaron? I talked to my attorney friend about it and he said that really the evidence should go through Aaron's lawyer."

Obie was using the scenario they'd talked about. She'd wanted to push him and ask him if he'd set her up. But they'd decided to tail Tallman after the card was in his possession. Chances were that he'd take it to the cartel and not back to his offices.

"I'll make sure the lawyer gets it," Tallman said.

"The last time you reassured me that this was probably nothing, I got shot at and had to spend two days in the swamp. So I think I'll keep it until I've spoken with Aaron."

Obie had gone off script and Xander tensed as Tallman snapped his hand out toward her. "Give it to me now."

"No."

He grabbed Obie, pulling her off the bench. He had his hand around her throat. Obie was clawing at him trying to get it off as his fingers tightened around her.

Xander saw red and left his cover, going straight for Obie and Tallman.

Obie knew the plan they had come up with, but from the moment she'd seen Tallman, she hadn't been sure she could go through with it. Now that she'd seen the pictures of him on the file and read the evidence that Aaron had gathered he seemed smarmy, dirty.

What an ass to think she was just going to hand over the card. That wasn't even the way that evidence was meant to handled. But he probably didn't expect her to think of that.

Pushing back on handing it over had seemed like a sort of good idea. Until he grabbed her off the table and started strangling her. His grip on her throat was hard and he kept tightening it. Her instinct was to try to claw his fingers open but he was stronger than she was.

She kicked backward, trying to knock him off balance, and connected with his leg. He stumbled and then he was pulled off of her. His hand tightened on her neck briefly and then he let go. She moved away from him, struggling to breathe, her eyes watering and as she looked back at Tallman she saw Xander had him pinned to the ground.

He was punching Tallman and Obie quickly realized that he might not stop. She ran forward to try to pull Xander off, but before she could get to him another man emerged from the path rushing toward them with his gun drawn. He fired at Xander, hitting him square in the chest and knocking him backward. Obie rushed to Xander's side as the other man stood over Tallman.

"This isn't handling it," the man said.

"I've got this, Bartolo. We can take care of both of them," Tallman said.

Obie held Xander close to her, trying to see put pressure on his wound but realized there was no blood. He mouthed the word *vest* to her.

He had worn a bulletproof vest, which made relief course through her body. For a moment she almost forgot the danger they were in. Bartolo Sanchez turned the gun toward her.

"The card now. I'm not going to argue with you."

She opened her purse, and as she did so Xander slipped his hand into hers and rolled her underneath him on the ground. She couldn't see what happened next, but she heard bullets being fired and Xander stayed on top of her until Van called an all clear.

Xander got to his feet and offered her his hand. Bartolo was injured on the ground close to them. Tallman had also been shot and was a few feet from his cousin-in-law. More men came streaming into the park from the DEA's office and the local cops.

"Are you okay?" she asked Xander.

"I'm fine. Probably bruised from the shot. You?"

Her throat hurt but she knew she'd be okay. "Yeah. That didn't go as planned."

Xander held her, gently moving his fingers over her throat before calling for a medic to examine her. "That's because someone didn't follow the plan."

"I know. I'm sorry but he was so… I just didn't want him to get away with it. I thought if I put up a bit of resistance it might make him do something stupid."

Xander rubbed his fingers over her brow and shook his head. "Or dangerous. He could have killed you."

"I had you watching over me. You'd never let him kill me."

He hugged her close but in his eyes she saw a fear that hadn't been there before. "I can't lose you."

She hugged him back. There were people bustling all around them but she didn't want to move away from him. "I feel the same."

"Do you?"

She nodded, afraid if she opened her mouth that

she'd blurt out that she loved him. That wasn't something she wanted to tell him in the midst of a shootout. She wanted time to talk to him alone when they both weren't injured and maybe were in a nice place.

"Xander, you two okay? The agents need to take a statement and you might want to go with them when they release your brother from jail," Van said as he came over to the two of them.

"Yeah."

"That was ballsy what you did, Obie. I should have guessed you weren't going to just let him walk away," Van said.

"I should have but I wasn't sure that we'd get any proof he was working with the cartel unless I pushed him."

"That you did. Did you know Bartolo was here?" Xander asked Van.

"Not until the old man on the park bench got up," Van said.

"I didn't really pay any attention to the people already here," Obie said.

"I did, but I'm surprised that it was Sanchez," Xander said.

Van nodded as he helped the two of them to their feet and the medic came and checked Obie out. "The information that Aaron got wasn't just going to reveal a crack in the organization. One of the other files has all the names of the men he'd uncovered. Bartolo's entire operation was at risk. He gave Tallman a chance to get it back but when he failed my guess is that he wasn't going to give him a second shot at losing it again."

Xander had to agree with Van. There was a lot at stake for La Familia Sanchez cartel. Aaron's information, along with the arrests of Tallman and Bartolo, should be enough to give the DEA a good shot at shutting them down.

Chapter 21

Van had them all brought back to the beach house in the gated community where they'd first come after the swamp. Xander had gone with Obie to the hospital, where she was treated and released. He had time while she was being examined to think about his actions. He'd saved her but barely pulled himself back from the rage that had been waiting to consume him.

The only other time he'd witnessed someone he loved being injured that way was Tony. And then Xander had turned into the violent and unpredictable person out of his own shame. He rubbed the back of his neck as he waited for Obie to come back from talking to Luna at the house.

He had changed. His anger was no longer directed at the world, and he knew his limits. Even if he went right to the edge with them.

And whether he wanted to admit it or not, both times the source of the change had been Aaron.

He wasn't sure he could just easily forgive his brother for dropping Obie into such a dangerous situation. But he was glad that he'd had the chance to meet her and that wouldn't have happened without Aaron.

the hair visible under the hat wasn't his natural black. There was no way to make himself shorter, but his jumpsuit was a couple of sizes too large and made him seem bulkier than he normally was.

They all had earpieces in except for Obie. So as soon as Luna left her at the car, she let them all know.

Xander moved with his rake to a position closer to the trail. He spotted Obie as she came walking toward him and the tables near the center of the park. She noticed him too but her gaze skimmed over him and she kept on walking.

He turned his back to the trail and made himself busy picking up some fallen branches and moving them to the bin he was using.

"She's almost in position," he said as she moved past his location.

"I've got eyes on Obie," Van said. "X, move around to the trees closer to the tables when you finish clearing those branches. Take your time when you get there. I want you in position as soon as Tallman arrives."

"Will do."

They were all tense until Kenji came on.

"Tallman's here. He appears to be alone. Coming toward your position now, Van."

It took all of his willpower to keep his head down and to keep working on the branches. He knew it was important not to break cover but his instincts screamed for him to tackle the other man to ground and beat the truth out of him.

Which wasn't how this was going to go down, so he kept working on clearing debris.

The door opened and the DEA agent who Xander hadn't met yet walked in first. A moment later Aaron was there. His brother was bigger than the last time they'd met, but then he was too. They'd both finished growing into the men they were today. When their eyes met, Xander hesitated for a moment and then went to his brother's side. Aaron pulled him into a hug. They held each other for a minute and then pulled back.

"I'm not sure I know what to say to you," Xander admitted.

"Well, let me start then. Thank you," Aaron said. "When my cover was blown and I was arrested I didn't know who else I could turn to. The other agents who worked with me would be in danger if one of them went to get the intel I'd collected."

"Yeah, so about the danger. You sent Obie in there blind."

"I'm sorry about that. But I had thought you'd be going instead of her," Aaron pointed out. "But you had to be shoved, didn't you?"

"I did. I wasn't ready to talk to you again," Xander said.

"I get it, little bro. I was the same way with everyone until last summer when Tony showed up here. We had a good long talk and I… Well, there's a lot more to discuss but we all need to stop avoiding going home."

"So you got arrested to make that happen?" Obie asked, coming over to them. She hugged Aaron and he hugged her back.

Xander watched them and saw that there was genuine affection between them. As much as she'd said

Aaron was a stranger to her, he clearly wasn't, not in a way that mattered.

"I'm sorry, Obs. I never meant for that to get so out of hand. But I hoped that Xander would keep you safe and he did. Still I shouldn't have sent you in like that," he said.

She nodded as she stepped back by Xander's side and slipped her hand into his. "You could have warned me. But I can't be upset with you. There were answers to questions about my parents on your SD card. I... thank you for that."

Aaron just nodded. "That was nothing. just information I had uncovered as I started working the case. Officer Wade remembered you and when I realized that my cover was being scrutinized I looked you up and got a job at your café."

"Why?" she asked.

"I was going to leave the SD card at work. Figured if something happened I'd have a chance to tell you to take it to Wade but I was arrested sooner than expected and the guards that were put on me worked for Sanchez so I couldn't speak freely when you visited. So I turned to my brother for help."

Seeing Aaron like this, Xander couldn't help sort of being astonished at him. "You've changed a lot since the SAS."

"Had to. It was either get my shit together or just give up and Quentins don't give up."

"Give up."

They both said the last part together.

"I missed you, bro. Heard you have turned into quite the legend as well," Aaron said.

Obie turned and gave him a look with her head tilted to the side. She had a bandage on her arm from a cut and bruises on her neck, but she was smiling at him, and he had never seen anyone more beautiful.

"Who said that?"

"Tony. Apparently Mom has been keeping tabs on you. One of her friends noticed you were at the G7 guarding someone from the US. They didn't know who it was."

"I was just helping out a friend," Xander said. The Secretary of State had requested him for the trip to England because he'd guarded her and her family before she'd taken the role and she trusted him to watch her kids while she was being guarded by the Secret Service.

"Yeah, sure," Aaron said.

Xander was embarrassed at the praise from his brother. Also surprised to hear his mom knew about his work. It was past time for him to take a visit home and renew the relationships that he'd severed out of fear. Aaron moved on to talk to Van and the rest of the team and he drew Obie away from them outside to the patio.

"It's nice to be outside and not running for our lives," she said.

"I agree. I like it here."

"Even though it's hot and things bite you," she teased.

He remembered his cranky breakdown when he'd

said that and started to laugh, then pulled her into his arms. "Even then. All of that means nothing to me when I have you in my arms."

"I like being in your arms, Xander," she said and then took a deep breath. "We haven't known each other for a long time but I feel like you are the person who knows me best."

He felt the same way. He glanced over his shoulder to make sure they were still alone. "I love you, Obie. I'd like to figure out a way for us to be together."

"I love you too, Xander," she said. She'd never thought she could be happy unless she'd changed everything about herself and became a woman who would fit in. But being in the swamp had made her face parts of herself that she'd forgotten she liked.

Xander played a big part in that. He'd just accepted her as she was, swamp girl mixed with suburbanite and all. "I want to figure out how to be together too. I'm also going to try to figure out me."

She'd spent a lot of time thinking about the fact that she didn't want to be a barista for the rest of her life. It was time to stop punishing herself for not going with Gator and to live a life that would be fulfilling to her.

And part of that meant finding a way to be with Xander. He meant the world to her, and she wasn't going to let him walk away again. She'd thought that by helping Aaron she'd find some peace with the decision she'd made the day that Gator had left but in truth it had been going back to the swamp with Xander that had saved her.

She had no idea what she wanted to do, but spending time in the swamp and studying the animals and plants that lived there appealed to her. She'd probably have to take a lot of classes to get a different degree, but she was okay with that. Those days in the swamp had reminded her that she was more important than keeping up appearances.

"I like you. What do you have to figure out?" he asked. "I like you the way you are."

He kissed her deeply and she couldn't help wrapping her arms and legs around him and kissing him back. When she lifted her head, she noticed his eyes were half-lidded and felt his erection between her legs.

"Thanks. But I think I'd like to go back to school and maybe work in the swamp," she said as he set her on her feet and took her hand, leading her away from the main house to the pool house.

"I can see you as a biologist," he said. "You'll be good at that. We might have to do long-distance for a while until I can find a job on the East Coast."

"Or I can go to school on the West Coast," she said.

But he shook his head. "No. You uprooted yourself and changed the course of your life once trying to become what your aunt Karen wanted for you. It's time for you to stay where you are. Let me come to you."

"I just don't want to lose you," she said. "I haven't been in love before, Xander, and I haven't felt this safe and sure of anything since my parents died. I want to be with you."

He hugged her close and he bent his head to hers.

His mouth was next to her cheek, and when he spoke, the words traveled no farther than the two of them.

"I won't let you go, Obie. You sort of make me feel okay not to be perfect and I've never had that in my life. When you are always competing and trying to be the winner... Well, I might have missed out on some things but I won't allow myself to miss out on you."

"Good. So we're agreed. I think as long as we both want to make this work we will," she said.

"We definitely will," he agreed. After all they'd survived two days in the swamp with just her skills, his wits and his backpack. They could manage living on opposite coasts until they got everything figured out.

He made love to her in the pool house and afterward they spent the evening with friends and family. Obie reached out and invited Aunt Karen, who was happy to see her safe and sound.

Aunt Karen showed up no questions asked. She took in Obie with her curly hair hanging around her shoulders. For a minute Obie felt her back go up, ready to defend herself but she didn't have to.

"You look happy. God, I don't think I've seen you this way since your mama died," Aunt Karen said, wiping her eyes with a tissue.

"I don't think I truly have been since then," she said, hugging her aunt. "I realize I never said thank you for that day you drove to Winter Haven and met me at the bus station."

"I should have taken you to look for Gator. I was just scared for you two and afraid that if you went back up there you might be in danger," she said.

"Were you suspicious of their accident too?"

"Of course. Your daddy was never meant to die in the swamp. That man knew it like the back of his hand and your mama and I were raised in it. I figured the best way I could keep you and Gator safe was to keep you with me and help you to blend in."

"Thank you for doing that. Did you ever hear anything from Gator?"

"I didn't. I am sorry I let him go. I just didn't know what else to do."

She hugged her aunt close, accepting that Aunt Karen had been keeping her safe the only way she knew.

"Thank you."

"It was nothing, Obie. You and Gator are my only kin—of course I had to keep you safe," she said.

She introduced her aunt to Xander and the two of them got on well. Obie looked around at the people in the backyard of the big house. The smell of the grill and the music playing made her realize how much of her life she'd spent hiding. She'd cut herself off from everything until now.

"I hear you might be my sister soon," Aaron said, coming up and handing her a beer, while draping one arm around her shoulder.

"I might," she said.

"I knew it. As soon as I met you I realized you and Xander would be good for each other," he said.

Which made her laugh. Xander came over to see what was so funny. "Aaron thinks he set us up."

"Oh, he did."

"Not like that. Like some kind of matchmaker," Obie said on a laugh.

"Hey, it worked. Do you think I could make a business out of it?" Aaron asked in a way that reminded her of Xander when he was teasing her.

"No," Obie and Xander both said at once.

Xander hugged her close. Aaron had put them in the right place, but it was those two days in the swamp, dodging bullets, crocs and alligators and weathering fierce rainstorms that had helped them fall in love. When there had only been the two of them and the elements, they'd had no choice but to lower the barriers they used to keep the world at arm's length.

Surviving the swamp had revealed the truth of who they were. The swamp girl and the beast man who wouldn't have even noticed each other on the streets of everyday Miami. Two soulmates who would have been ships crossing in the night, if not for Aaron and his life-threatening favor.

* * * * *

*Watch for the next exciting installment
in the Price Security series
coming in October 2024!*